I0548129

She struggled to her feet and reacher over to her knitting basket. She inspected the sharp points of two of the needles to make certain that there was no material attached to them, snatched her pillow from the bed and pulled a clean sheet out of the dresser drawer. She almost burst into tears as she walked back into the kitchen to find Lena staring at the table as though it were a slab in the city morgue.

"Did you wash it good?" she asked sharply, masking her feelings.

"Uh huh."

"Good. Now here, help me."

The two women moved slowly, covering the table with the sheet as though they were performing a ritual. Miss Rabbit placed the pillow at one end and two chairs, stirrup style, at both sides of the table at the other end. Efficiently, she checked the back door lock, made certain that the shades were drawn and came finally to stand in front of Lena.

"Now you have to lay up here, Lena . . . 'n spread your legs, just like you was gon' have a baby, in order for me to do what I got to do. But first, lemme ask you again, are you sho' you don't want to have this . . .?"

A slow trickle of tears slid down Lena Daniels' high cheekbones as she lay on the table. "Yes, yes . . . I want to have the baby, but we can't afford it, Miss Rabbit . . . we can hardly feed the ones we got."

ODIE HAWKINS

THE BUSTING OUT OF AN ORDINARY MAN

Copyright © 1985, 2012 by Odie Hawkins

Front cover photo by Zola Salena-Hawkins,
www.flickr.com/photos/32886903@N02

ISBN: 978-1-5040-3582-8

Distributed in 2016 by Open Road Distribution
180 Maiden Lane
New York, NY 10038
www.openroadmedia.com

For my sister,
Louise,
And all her children

THE BUSTING OUT OF AN ORDINARY MAN

Chapter 1
Monday

"My dearest Kwendi,

I hope you are past your depression by now,   your last letter bothered me very much. I almost feel ashamed sometimes to admit that my love for you is so great, so profoundly tuned to what goes through you that the vibes from your letter told me that you were about to do something uncool.

Please baby   don't. You know how badly they want to wipe your strong, beautiful black ass away (you know what I almost said, don't you, smile).

Kwendi, seriously, don't do anything that would foul you up, the lawyers are doing all they can, your defense money is steadily coming in, people have become more concerned and aware of how rank the shit is here   like, yesterday it was you, tomorrow it might be anyone, even one of the apathetic ones. At any rate, all I'm saying is that I love you, googobs, I miss you and, in order for us to ever be together again, to fight the battles with this crazy, weird, hypocritical racist ass society that we know have to be fought, to make the sweet black babies we've been talking through that screen about for the last five years, to do anything that we've planned, then You Must Be Alive. You know they want to kill you, baby   you know that, and all they need is any kind of excuse, any kind.

I'm not trying to tell you to submit to anything, to be less than the man you are, or anything like that. I just want you to be cool and be careful.

Kwendi, I love you so much.

Because we both decided a long time ago, that we would be fair and honest with each other about our feelings, I don't feel any need to hold back, to conceal this terrible hunger I feel inside for you.

Maybe the season has something to do with it (smile) fall always makes me feel more nostalgic than usual. I took a walk in the park yesterday, in search of some leaves to kick around, and spent an hour going through as many moments in our relationship as I could remember.

Kwendi, I love you so much.

The feeling gushes up in me, so strong at times that I feel almost like I felt the first time we made love. Remember me, baby? The eighteen year old innocent that you didn't want to make love to because you thought it would be too heavy a scene for my head. Remember?

I laugh out loud sometimes, thinking about us   two dumb eighteen year old fools who almost respected each other to death, you, afraid to 'seduce' a sister because you felt that that might be considered counterrevolutionary or some such thing, and me, with my stupid self, almost letting you get away with it.

10

Just think, if we had known what was going to go down, we would have been a lot less careful and maybe I would have your child now

Kwendi, I miss you so much. I feel so distracted, so alone, at times.

I'm takin' care maximum business in every direction, feeling strong, but the thought that my lover, my man, is locked away from me weighs me down sometimes. But who in the hell am I to complain?

Many sisters might hesitate, I think, to write the man in their lives a letter like this, especially if he were in the joint. I am not now nor do I think I could ever be that image-ridden sister who refuses to let her carefully arranged 'Afro' mask fall away, telling herself, being rational, that her man only wants to hear nothing but the safe, pleasant, groovy things.

Emotionally, we're both in prison and I can't help spilling my guts out to the only person in the world who understands me.

As a writer, when I can write it out to you, spell words, say to my dearest, dearest Kwendi, darling I love you and know that you, as a fellow writer, as my man, will find more than anyone else could hope to find in those three words ... when I can do that, it makes my nights more bearable.

I'm carrying on our people's work as best I can without you. Djenkasi, Abdul, Nici, Maisha and a few others remain the hard, strong core   The others remain more or less constant.

The main problem we have is lack of leadership. I know what you're going to say in your next letter, that we should all be leaders, but, for some reason, it just doesn't quite work out that way. The theater section of the group has started a thing they call G.D.! ('Gittin' Down!'), and it's being given a good response by the community.

Several other projects are working out quite well also, I'll

11

tell you more about them on visiting day.

Does it seem strange to you that yesterday we were eighteen and now we are both twenty-three?

Time seems to stand still or pass itself by.

I'm afraid I must end this one now, leaving so much unsaid that we may need another lifetime to cover half of it, but it doesn't matter, my spirits are high and my love is strong. With all my best love,
Lubertha, your Kush

P.S. I'm sure you've heard about Baby June, but you'd have to see him to really believe the change   unreal!"

Monday evening, the dreariest day of the week anywhere, but especially in the Afro-American ghetto; people, having taken hangovers and other symptoms of a fast weekend to their individual sections of the plantations around town, return, the weight of four more days (and maybe five) of clock punching and lockstepping ahead of them before the eagle flies.

Mrs. Nelda Washington, better known as Big Momma, shuffled her elbows, recrossed her arms and spat into the Maxwell House coffee can at her feet, barely paying any mind to the receptacle, being so certain of her aim, and turned her full attention back to the people passing back and forth on the sidewalk in front of her. She knew them all, some since babyhood. Lubertha, on her way to the mailbox with another letter to   what was that child's name? Kwenni? Kwanjo? Kuwani? Something like that.

Shame that they threw him away in jail like that

"Hi, Big Momma, how you doin'?"

Big Momma shot another swift stream of snuff juice into the can before answering, slowly, as was her habit.

"Ooooohhhh, I don't know, Lubertha, passable, I guess
Wid the good Lawd's blessins I'll live."

12

"Well, you take it easy," Lubertha answered graciously, "I'm goin' down to the corner, you want anything?"

"Nawww, cain't say that I do, daughter, just now . . . Bessie promised t' brang me some snuff when she got home. Thanks anyway."

Lubertha waved and kept on, her head held high, her back straight. Big Momma studied her movement for a few steps, recalling the Lubertha Franklin she knew from five years back.

Lawwwwd in Heaven, she thought, nodding her head slightly,   sin 'n a shame the thangs that happen to people

Girl cain't be but twenny   twenny-two at the most, and she's got them ol' hard lines 'round her mouth like a woman thirty.

Well, guess that's what happens when you lose your man.

She sighed deeply and nodded to a strange face that happened to look up and see her. The face, surprised at the neighborly gesture, frowned and picked up his pace.

Funny how much afraid peoples is when you try to be friendly.

Big Momma shivered, looked up at the narrow patch of gray sky that hung over her street and, at that moment, thought about her husband.

Wonder if Booker went t' Heaven? Nawww, not likely, not much hell as *that* man raised. Thought he was the greatest thang in pants, wid his moonshinin', his sly ways, and all that pride he had 'cause his Daddy had named him Booker, after Booker T.

Another autumn breeze eased through, bringing goose pimples out on her fleshy arms. She spat again and pulled her sweater a little tighter around her shoulders, her mind slipping away from her dead husband, dead for twelve years, to the thought of the hard winter she saw ahead in the clouds above.

13

She stood up slowly, a darker version of Ethel Waters, bracing her hands on her arthritic knees as she prepared to close down her window.

During all seasons, Big Momma sat . . . in the spring, summer and early fall, on the top level of the stone porch jutting out from her apartment building, in the late fall and winter, behind the glass pane, seeing and taking everything in.

She closed the window, a can of soup and some crackers already prepared, mentally, and stood at the window for a minute, her knuckles pressed down on the window ledge as she watched Baby June stride up the street selling the Muslim newspaper, *The Bilalian*.

"Baby June!" she called to him.

"Yes ma'am!" he answered, as though on cue, turning her way with fluid quickness.

"Brang me one o' them!"

Baby June smiled slightly as he tripped up the stone steps to the porch, a paper already folded and held out for delivery. "Here you are, Sister Washington," he said, leaning over from the edge of the porch to hand her the paper.

Big Momma reached out for the paper with her left hand as she fumbled down into her apron pocket with her right.

"There's no charge for you, Sister Washington," Robert 30X said graciously, knowing that her coins were, as usual, short.

"Well, thank ya, Baby   uhhh   Robert . . . Lawwwd! I just cain't never remember to call you nothin' but Baby June."

"Oh, that's quite all right, Sister Washington, quite all right."

Big Momma smiled at Robert 30X, formerly called Baby June in his dope fiend salad days, feeling a maternal pride in his superneatness.

Too bad Sister Sadie didn't live long enough to see the change happen, Big Momma thought.

14

Robert 30X stood at respectful attention, his heels together, feet spread at a precise thirty-five degree angle.

"Thanks again, now   babeee ... Robert! I'm gon' read this with my mind open, just like you asked me to do."

"I appreciate that, Sister Washington, the Honorable Elijah Muhammad taught us that only an open mind is ready for the truth. And please remember the offer I made to you, about attending services in the mosque, is still open   All you have to do is just let me know when you'd like to go, and we'll have a car pick you up and bring you back."

"That'd be really nice, Bobby ... really nice, soon as I'm feelin' a lil' better, I just might gon' on over there."

"Anytime, Sister Washington, anytime," Robert 30X sang out as he bowed slightly in her direction and skipped away down the steps to intercept Lubertha, returning from the mailbox.

Big Momma closed the window again, watching Robert 30X match Lubertha stride for stride as she dug down into her jeans for the price of a paper. She lowered her shade and pulled the old, heavily brocaded curtains together and shuffled away from the window, fumbling to put her reading glasses on, hung on a string around her neck   placed the paper on her all purpose kitchen table.

Opening a can of chicken noodle soup, counting out five saltine crackers and measuring a short glass of milk into a tall Mason jar, she read aloud the headline of the paper, "Raise your own food, Black man!"

Phyllisine Evans looked over the counter at the little dude wandering around the store, his nose bleeding a thin trickle of snot that he absently wiped off on the forearm of his sweater from time to time.

Watching him pretend that he was just a window shopper, inside the store, made her smile.

"May I help you, sir?" she asked in her most officious voice.

He looked up at her shyly, trying to be hip, and answered, "Nawwww, I was just lookin'."

Frontin' it off, huh? she smiled at him knowingly, and dipped into the oatmeal cookie jar, pulled out two of them and handed them across to him.

The little boy looked surprised for a second, snatched the cookies from her hands with one greedy motion and ran out of the store wolfing on one as he went.

Phyllisine shook her head sadly, knowing that he was probably eating his first meal of the day.

She backed into the high stool behind the counter, her eyes still on the door, the jangling bell above it, her thoughts still on the little boy.

Well, at least mine don't have to go through that. Maybe Momma made a good choice after all.

She gazed around the store, a momma 'n poppa affair with two aisles and a small meat display counter.

Yeahhhh, maybe Momma did do the right thing.

Her stepfather, never called anything but ol' man Jackson, the geechee, clanged through the door with a crate on his shoulder.

"Why don'cha git off that stool 'n come 'elp me?!" he called to her in his West Indian singsong.

Phyllisine, her thoughts jarred by his sudden entrance, stumbled as she dismounted the stool.

"Huh! What did you say?" she asked him.

"What's the matter, ya hard o' 'earin'? I said, come 'elp me!"

She skirted the edge of the counter, grinding her teeth together   even after five years, she still found it hard to understand ol' man Jackson sometimes, especially when he got excited and his Barbadan dialect thickened.

16

He was already inside the store with the crate; what did he want? She stood in front of him, hands clasped behind her back, a question mark on her face.

" 'Urry up oat dere 'n git that large brunn bag in the front seat o' the truck,   make it quick else the dahm thieves'll bee'cha to it."

Phyllisine hurried out to his many dented pickup truck, rubbing her arms, suddenly chilled by the late afternoon cool. She struggled to pull the shopping bag from the cab of the truck, cursing under her breath.

" 'Urry it up, Phyllisine! We ain't got ahl day!" ol' man Jackson yelled as he rushed to pull the burglar guard mesh across the front of the store.

Phyllisine muscled the sack of potatoes out and struggled into the store with them. She looked hatefully at her stepfather's back as he quickly removed the day's take from the register, scurried around, checking the alarm system, turning off lights.

"Where you want me to put these?" He turned to her and, with that surprising burst of warmth that caught her off balance so often, said, "Ohhh, just leave 'em dere, ahl'll dump 'em in the bin tomorra'."

She watched him carefully reach into the meat display counter and give a final pat to the long, meat-loaf shaped piece of sausage he had brought in, that and the two dozen half-stale steaks cleverly covering each other, the result of dealing with the neighborhood dope fiends.

Damn, he really moves quick for an old dude, she thought, watching him scurry around one last time.

"Ahl set t' go?"

Phyllisine nodded affirmatively in the dim light, anxious to get outside, to find out what had gone down during the time she had been locked up.

"Where's your mother?" he asked abruptly as he slammed

17

the guard mesh together and padlocked it.

"She's upstairs with the kids."

Ol' man Jackson frowned slightly, went over to the curb to make certain his truck was locked and returned to Phyllisine standing at the foot of the steps leading to their apartment over the store, growling, "You mean t' say thot she left ya dohn'ere ahl by yerself in the store?"

"Not all day, she was down in the mornin' and then I spelled her in the afternoon."

Ol' man Jackson, frowning, started up the steps mumbling, "Ah don' lak dat, should be a grown up in the store at ahl times, ahl times."

He was at the top of the steps before he realized she wasn't behind him.

"Ya comin' up or not?" he asked, his question as blunt and gruff as the rest of his actions.

"Uhhh, nawwww, not right now. I'm gon' walk over to Mary Jo's for awhile."

"Well, don' stay too long, ya know 'ow ya mother gets when ya leave 'er alone with the kids too long."

"I ain't gon' be long," she answered, easing away down the street. He entered the hallway of their building and slammed the door behind him.

Should be a grown up in the store at ahl times, ahl times. She corrected her thought. Shit! What was she, if she wasn't grown? What did it take beyond having two babies and being eighteen years old to be considered a grown up? She dug her hands into her pockets, stepping into the brisk evening breezes, having no definite place to go.

Mary Jo's was a lame excuse. Mary had gotten strung out two years ago and disappeared, but neither Mr. Jackson nor her mother knew, they didn't care to know, being so busy trying to make ends meet.

Daddy! Maybe I'll run into him, he's usually someplace

around the Dew Drop 'round about this time.

She walked a little faster, feeling happier about the possibility of seeing her father.

"Heyyy, Phyllisine! Phyllisine!" Billy Woods called to her from across the street. She watched him, a neutral expression on her face, dodge around and between cars, to reach her.

Billy Woods, almost a brother to her, from living in the same neighborhood so long, she felt   but somehow the point was never fully conveyed to Billy.

"Where you on your way?" he asked, trying to be cool about it.

She almost lied but thought better of it, why lie?

"I was just takin' a lil' walk."

"Any place special?"

"Uhhh, not really," she answered, looking away into the distance.

"I'm goin' your way."

"I'd really much rather be by myself," she said coldly.

Billy's eyes wandered over her body before he coughed deep in his throat, trying to cover up the slap to his macho.

"Right on! I can dig where you comin' from," he replied lamely, trying to save face. "Everybody needs some time to be by theyselves."

Phyllisine turned away from him, feeling a little embarrassed for him, but felt she was doing the right thing. After all, she didn't dig him, she knew exactly what he was after, and she wasn't going to give him any   so why jive? Billy Woods, like most of the dudes in and around the neighborhood wanted to cop Phyllisine   Why not? The damage had already been done, and what was left just had to be pure jelly.

Billy looked wistfully at her full, taut buttocks as she strolled away.

Phyllisine, aware that he was following her movement, tried

19

to tighten the roll of her hips, but failed.

These jiveass motherfuckers! All they want is a piece o' pussy, ain't gon' do shit to help with your kids or anything, bunch a' chickenshit niggers! Momma's right! Niggers ain't shit!

She walked past Big Momma's window, crossed the street in front of Lubertha's apartment building, thought about May-flower's death as she passed his building and turned the corner.

The Dew Drop Inn glared at her from the end of the block, drew her like a neon magnet.

What do I say to him if I run into him? she asked herself, slowing down despite the deepening chill.

She never felt really capable of handling herself when the mood came down on her, the mood to see her father; long ago, when she had been pregnant with a rapist's baby, her father came around with three other men, asking her to tell them who had raped her. She never told them because she didn't know, but she did know that Chu-man was the father of the second one, the one they had had trying to forget the traumatic experience of the rape.

Chu-man   Chu-man   the thought of him made her jam her hands deeper into her pockets. What had he said in his last letter? "Soon as I get out, we going to get it together, for real!"

She peeked into the bar hesitantly, blinking her eyes in the semi-dark.

"He ain't here, honey!" a buxom woman in a champagne colored Afro wig called out to her. "I'm lookin' for 'im my-self, wid his raunchy ass!"

Phyllisine ignored the raucous laughter that spilled out at her, turned and started back home.

Of all people, why did I have to see that bitch of his!

"Hey looka'here, Miss Lady ... lemme buy you a drink?"

20

a tricky voiced, superfly type sang out to her softly from the interior of his gangster whitewalls at the curb.

She nodded no-thanks quickly and began walking faster, getting away from the sly looks, the chilliness of the air and the rapidly descending darkness.

Too bad that ol' man Jackson ain't like my real father so cool, so smooth, so hip. Oh well, I guess you can't have everything. At least we got a roof over our heads and food every day. Momma knows what she's doin'.

Rudolph Little, alias Rappin' Rudy, fumbled with three of his books, dropped them on the sidewalk as he made his way down the steps from his third floor apartment, cursed, picked them up and rushed past Phyllisine to get the 7:15 downtown.

"Hi, Rudy!" Phyllisine spoke coyly to him as he dashed past.

"Oh, hey Phyll, what's happenin'!" he replied, not really caring to know pre-law, the current government scandals involving so many lawyers, the American judicial set-up, decisions of the Supreme Court from 1925 to 1965, and a dozen jurisprudential matters on his brain, in addition to the fact that he was running late again. He was at the corner before he fully realized that he had spoken to Phyllisine.

Wowwww! I gotta slow down a lil' taste! For Phyllisine? he probed himself as the bus approached, nawww, not for her, fine as she is, for myself She ain't into nothin', with two crumbcrushers and no ambition.

Yeahhh, I better slow down for my own good.

He mounted the bus steps with two jumps, dropped his coins into the fare box and dashed to the back of the bus, determined to read one more chapter before class.

The bus moved along, lurching and jerking, making it harder for him to concentrate.

21

Miss Rabbit sat across from Lena Daniels at her kitchen table, sipping strong, black coffee and listening to Lena, cocking her left eyebrow into an inverted V from time to time, as Lena rapped to her about a developing problem.

"So, that's why   you see, I just can't have no mo' babies, not right in through here, anyway."

Miss Rabbit countered her bold, questioning plea for help with an oblique glance at the sampler above her kitchen stove. God Bless This Home.

"God Bless This Home," she read slowly, moving her full lips slightly. "So, now   whatchu wont me t' do, Lena?"

Lena Daniels twisted her gold wedding band around twice, three times, five times, nervously. "I want you to help me out, Miss Rabbit . . . I know you can, I just don't know what t' do," she added, a pathetic curl to her tone.

"How you know I can help you?" Miss Rabbit asked sharply, her eyes narrowed in a threatening way. "Somebody tol' you I could?"

"Oohhh no, no, Miss Rabbit! ain't nobody tol' me nothin' about what you can   uhh   could do, nobody!"

"Well then, if that's the case, what made you come t' me with your problem?"

Lena Daniels' eyes darted from one corner of the room to another, settled down finally on the coffee cup in front of her as she spoke in a low monotone. " 'Member a few years back, when Jim was messin' off all his money 'n foolin' 'round in the streets?"

Miss Rabbit released a satisfied smile at the memory of her constructive interference. "Daggoned right I remember, got 'im squared away quite nicely, as I recollect."

" 'Member how you blessed Jimbo 'n Suki-man? after they came down with whatever it was they had, and they got well   had the doctor all confused and everything."

Miss Rabbit's smile broadened, showing seven dark, empty

22

spaces strategically arranged in her teeth. "Uhm huhn, 'course I remember all that," she answered slyly.

"Miss Rabbit, I just can't have this baby!" Lena burst out, her eyes glassy with frustration and tears.

Miss Rabbit leaned toward her, patted her arm maternally, reassuringly, sat back in her chair, lit a cigarette and smoked half of it before saying anything.

"Lena," she began heavily, "you know, doin' somethin' like you talkin' about doin' is damn serious."

Lena nodded solemnly in agreement. "I know it is, Miss Rabbit. I know it is, but we got six now, and you know how hard times is."

Miss Rabbit nodded in turn, stabbed her cigarette out and lit another one. She took four slow, deliberate drags. "Tell ya what, honey   today is Monday, lemme thank 'n pray on it for a couple days."

A look of deep gratitude washed across Lena Daniels' full face as she reached across the table impulsively, to grab Miss Rabbit's hand.

"Don't be gettin' all het up 'n everythang!" she spoke in a semi-stern voice, "I didn't say I'd do anythang, I just said I'd pray on it."

Lena's look of gratitude became a bit more guarded, but refused to fully slip away. "I understand, Miss Rabbit whatever you decide will be o.k. with me," she said and uncoiled herself from the chair.

Miss Rabbit took a full, professional look at her waistline. " 'Bout three full months gone, huh?"

"Just about to the day."

"Well," Miss Rabbit rose with a sigh, "that ain't too turrible bad."

She shuffled the few steps to the back door with Lena, her arm draped lovingly around the younger woman's waist.

"You know somethin', Miss Rabbit," Lena said to her as

23

she was about to take her first step out of the door.

"What's that, honey?"

"Sometimes   sometimes I wish you had raised me."

Miss Rabbit's stern-gentle features softened. "Gon' girl! git outta here 'n mind them chillun o' yourn!" She scolded her gruffly, ill at ease with Lena's thought.

Lena smiled, understanding.

Miss Rabbit watched her make it down to the alley before closing the door.

She shuffled back over to the kitchen stove, reheated the coffee, poured another cup, sat down at the table and began to cry. A quiet trail of tears spilled down alongside her nose, over her high cheeks, as she wrestled with the deep problem of taking the life from Lena Daniels, of destroying something that nobody but God had a right to destroy.

"Ohhh my Lawwwd, please give me a sign   she moaned, and lowered her head to the table to pray.

Lubertha's eyes wandered from face to face, smiling at one, nodding to another. There were times when she hated the Club's meetings without Kwendi, the way the brothers and sisters looked at her as though she were some kind of martyred black ghost.

She listened to Nici run up one list of financial figures and down another, explaining in detail exactly what expenditures had been made, what this and what that was all about.

Charlie Tucker stood as soon as she had finished, to give out the latest on Kwendi's case, what progress had been made and how. The job had formerly been Lubertha's, but over the years it had become too rough for her to handle emotionally   to stand at meetings and announce to the world that her man was in a deep bind, that she was in limbo and that it was likely to be that way for years.

She caught Ojenkasi looking at her, a soft gleam in his eyes,

24

and smiled pleasantly, neutrally, in his direction. He always seems to be looking at me these days, she reflected, gearing herself for the Political Awareness section of the meeting, her contribution.

In nine other places in the city, at staggered times, this same kind of meeting was taking place ... with certain allowances for personality differences, the meeting was the same. The police-oppressors called them cell meetings of subversives, conspirators, and tried to keep tabs on them whenever they could. The membership simply called itself the Club, and came to learn a few truths, gain some insight and awareness, hoping eventually to put it all together in such a fashion that they would effect some profound changes in their neighborhoods, the city, the state and perhaps the country.

The Club had almost been killed off during the first three years of its existence, before it learned not to publicize its aims, to give the enemy guidelines   but now it stood strong, vital and thriving. Kwendi's spirit giving it life.

Lubertha stood quickly at the conclusion of Charlie Tucker's report, in tune with the policy they had established to prevent business from dragging on and on. "This evening, sisters and brothers, goin' on with how some of the bullshit operates in this country   I would like to cover briefly three specific areas that are very important to all of us. I haven't really labeled each of the areas because they're all interrelated   politics, money and food."

She paused to study her notes for a couple seconds, pursing her lips thoughtfully, mindful of a few things that Kwendi had laid on her in a recent letter. "Give them as much hip information as they can stand, baby   black folks have been given enough entertainment and rhetoric,   what we all need is some correct information   information, information and more information, something that will act as a true agent for change."

25

"First of all," she continued, "on the political side, I don't think I have to go into a whole bunch of examples to show how rotten the political structure of the country is at this point in time. Even the corrupt newspapers owned by the corrupt politicians find themselves being forced to tell the truth because everyone knows the truth nowadays, well, at least those who admit that they know the truth.

"As you all remember, in our last meeting we discussed the reasons why the political structure started off stanky and got progressively rotten as time went on. That was back in the days of Georgie Wash-in-ton the uh ruhhh father of our country."

She paused to allow the laughter that her sarcastic tone of voice provoked to die down.

"The span of time we have covered goes from then to now," she held up a newspaper clipping of one of the president's latest lies, "but the prerequisite, the conditions needed for wrongdoin' in government have always existed, they've been encouraged, the founding 'fathers' made certain of that. The only changes that've been made over the years is that the corruption is more sophisticated, more ruthless, more corrupt now.

"Two of the greatest reasons why corruption has always been a part of the American political scheme of things concerns, first of all, money, and secondly, money. We could reverse those two things and still wind up, probably, with the same hill o' beans."

She checked Chico Daddy and Chiyo Mungu's expressions out closely to determine whether or not her message was getting through. She knew, from experience, if they were understanding it all, then she was over.

Chiyo's puzzled frown told her that she'd have to go a little deeper, in a simpler way.

"Let's step back in time a lil' bit, to when the contracts

26

and deals were being made. One of the things that the dealer made certain of when he was passin' out the contracts was that the dudes with the most bread got the biggest cut of whatever was being passed out . . . them that's got shall get. Them that's not shall lose, so Billie Holiday said in her song.

"Despite all the rhetoric about this being a democracy 'n all, it didn't start off that way and it hasn't become one yet

as a matter of fact, it's lookin' more and more like it's not about to happen every day."

Chiyo's frown eased slightly.

"O.k., I started off about money, power and food. If you check the situation out closely, you'll see the people who've always been in power, those few rich dudes who decide how much everything is goin' to cost, the ones who have always had the means to manipulate prices . . . and since we all have to eat, the greatest manipulation has been with food prices.

"Yeahhh, I know, we can talk about steel, lumber and a whole bunch of other things, but they wind up being spinoffs from the basic manipulations."

She paused again, to watch Ojenkasi walk over and shake Sherman from a light nap, or was he nodding? There were rumors going around about him.

"Now then," she continued, smiling briefly at Ojenkasi, "on the basis of what we've gone over before, we know that, early on in the game, the power structure of this country has practiced dollar imperialism, backed up by superior bullshit and a greater lack of scruples than almost any other country in modern times. Including England.

"Those of us who've paid close attention to how and why this country has messed around in the internal affairs of other countries know that usually the reason was for the benefit of the rich and the rippin' off of the poor. To use an example, a lot of people would like to believe that the American war fought against the Vietnamese people was to prevent the

27

spread of communism from the north of Vietnam to the south. Meanwhile, the president of this country was over in Big Bad Red China, drinkin' toasts with Mao because the money people here, fed up with that rhetoric about a jive Bamboo Curtain, had told him, look asshole! git your jiveass over there and set up some trade agreements with those people . . . eight-hundred million Chinese are dyin' for a Coca Cola and a stick of Beechnut chewin' gum.

"And so he went, just like he was 'sposed to go, because Big Business sent him.

"Meanwhile, back in the war, which was being fought for control of the dope trade in Cambodia, Laos and Vietnam . . . ."

BoBo spoke out, a skeptical look on his serious, dark face, "For the dope trade, sister?!"

"That's right, brother   for the dope trade. Doesn't it stand to reason? Dig it   practically every commercial enterprise in this country is fought over, or for, in one sense of the word or another. Now let's face it, heroin is big, big business," she paused briefly to stare pointedly at Sherman's dreamy expression. "If any of us in this room had a kilo of heroin that we wanted to kill our people off with, all we'd have to do is get together with those who are tryin' to do it anyway and make a sale.

"Two to one, whoever bought it would probably cheat us in the deal and have us ripped off, to seal the deal. But that's to be expected. All I'm really tryin' to say, by way of example, is that dope dealin' is probably the biggest and best business in the world   you got a built-in consumer market, and the profits are fantastic. Why wouldn't they fight a war over that? Call it America's secret opium war if you want to."

She paused again, theatrically, to let her message sink in, feeling proud of the enlightened look she had put on BoBo's face. "I think I've drawn enough parallels between money

28

and power, that's not too hard to put together. I'd like to wind up with the connection of food to all this . . . ."

She felt tempted to say "Kwendi says," but erased the thought, anxious not to mummify what he was saying to her in letters, besides, he'd told her many times about the dangers of the cult thing.

"If you check out the price on items like bread 'n milk, for example, you'll see that they've usually been jacked up unmercifully after one of this country's wars   the reason being, after the power elite have made all they can make on guns 'n bullets, and there's not too much more to be made on other items, the one stable source for a ripoff is food, so they add three or four pennies more to items we have to have and continue makin' up, keepin' our cost of livin' high so that they can cover their inflated standard of livin'."

She probed the attentive faces for a sign of disagreement as she talked, feeling a twinge of guilt at not being able to really say in words something about the concepts, the ideas that Kwendi was laying on her from his deep introspection in prison.

She came to the end of her remarks with a solid bit of advice, "Know where they're comin' from, or else you might get fooled," and sat down, feeling vaguely dissatisfied with her presentation. For some reason, no matter what she said or how she said it, it was always a dim shadow of the kind of muscular intensity Kwendi had going.

Abdul Aboud stood next, to give a progress report on their alliance with three Chicano groups who were modeling an organization after theirs. Lubertha studied the fiercely carved lines in Abdul's face and wondered, for the first time, what his name had been before he changed it.

The beginning of the Club, the agony that made it necessary, the guidelines established, the early days of arguments about what they would or could accomplish, flashed through

29

her consciousness as she listened to the heavy rise and fall of brother Abdul's voice. A sudden, deepfelt sense of hope lessness overwhelmed her for a moment . . . she lowered her head, afraid that the feeling would show in her eyes, betray everything they were trying to accomplish. What the hell did it matter? she asked herself, if they had cleaned all the dope peddlers out of the neighborhood and had some slimy politician take all the credit for it.

What did it matter that her little seminars on American politics taught young brothers and sisters more than they would ever learn in any American school about the real nature of the dominant white power force? Or that they had established sections in each one of the Clubs that dealt with Art, Music, Ourstory, Drama, Mathematics, Sociology, the Politics of Revolutions and how to make them work. In addition to having worked on each other, sharpening their sense of brotherness with real sacrifices for each other, like sending Rudy to school.

None of it seemed to matter, she thought sadly,   none of it, so long as the world they were living in was threatened to be polluted out of existence, any coming month now. Not something purely black, white, yellow, brown or any other color, despite the fact that the white boy, with his misguided ideas about what manhood was all about, was largely responsible for it.

No, this was something greater than they were   a little bunch of Afro-Americans wanting human rights, this was a planet rights thang, and she hated being forced to only deal with a thin, thin slice of the whole thing.

Nici Miles nudged Maisha, pointed at Lubertha with her eyelashes, Maisha nodded back, aware of Lubertha's state of mind, saddened beyond words for her sister's hurt . . . After all, how many Kwendis were there in the world?

The meeting went on

Rudy slouched down in his seat, half a mind on what might be going on at the Club's meeting, half a mind on what the little dull-eyed Jewish guy with the tweed sports jacket and the expensive pipe was saying.

He glanced around at his classmates, their shiny blue eyes riveted on the instructor's movements as though he were an A+ in slow motion. His attention wandered into the seat two aisles to the right of him, right up between the milk-fed thighs of Dora Hirschberger   and then sped away, guilt ringing down the curtain.

This was definitely not what the Club was sending him to school for!

He smiled to himself and scribbled a flurry of notes, what a helluva idea! His own, he thought proudly, to send Club members off to school, to use their talents in as many ways as possible to help the community. The idea had blossomed in him during Kwendi's third trial, attended to by a jive black lawyer who had been damned near shamed into dealing with the case, threatened might've been a different way to describe his involvement.

It was at that point that he began to persuade, first Kwendi and then the membership. Rather than just be some damned gang, he had argued, whipping asses and taking names, why not become doctors, lawyers, artists, professionals working for the Club's causes? Which had to be the people's causes, 'cause that's who they were.

He frowned at the memory of some of the arguments, some of the opposition the sisters and brothers had given him.

"Awww, what the fuck you tryin' to pull, Rudy!? All you wanna do is take a freebie on our backs."

Yeahhh, the obstacles had been there, but eventually, with Kwendi backing the idea and the membership falling in line, they had managed to stick four sisters and brothers into school. Law, economics, Kwendi's idea   "We ought to

31

know how money makes things function up in here." Kwendi Jones, beautiful brother. Ourstory, political science, and they were trying to groom a brother and sister for medical school; that was going pretty slow because of the expense, but hopefully, within the next few years, they would have Club doctors, lawyers, economists, hip dudes from the block with more than just degrees, pieces of paper, more than an "education," they would have a sense of commitment to the community that sponsored them.

He straightened up in his seat, suddenly conscious that he was a Club member and that he had a rep to maintain. The Club's scholarship people, they called themselves, and worked harder because they had pride in that.

Rudy wrinkled his forehead, trying to concentrate harder, to scratch all other intruding thoughts.

Wonder where Phyllisine was going? Oh well

"And now, class   will you please place all of your notes and books under your seats, we're going to have a lil' quiz, call it twenty questions, if you like   hah hah hah . . . ."

Rudy placed his books under his desk, thought of keeping his small notepad concealed under his left forearm, but decided against it. What the fuck! I can go through this shit blindfolded, with minimum output, and still get a B. Why cheat?

He folded his hands on his desk and waited grimly for the multiple choice questionnaire to be passed out. Even with a full time gig and a thousand 'n one other things to worry about, school was a sop, the hardest part was making it to class on time.

He bent over his questionnaire as soon as it was dropped on his desk and mentally marked the first ten correctly yeahhh, school was a sop.

Fergy Smith shifted his weight slightly, trying to ease out of the depression on his side of the bed, as he listened to his

32

woman's movements in the kitchen. Of all the goddamned, fucked up things to be afflicted with, what the hell could be worse than to have a bad back? He rolled his head from side to side, feeling swamped by self pity and anger.

I knew I should've asked somebody to help me lift that fuckin' sack, but nawww, not me, not ol' strong nuts Smith.

Lucille popped through the bedroom door with a glass of water. "Here, Fergy   it's time for your pills."

He frowned at the thought of swallowing the two horse-sized tablets he had to take every night. "Damn, Lucille! Why can't we skip 'em tonight, baby?"

Lucille placed a fist on one well-endowed hip and moved the water glass inches closer. "Now, Fergy   you know what the doctor said!"

He reached out reluctantly for the glass of water with one hand, and to the pills on his night table with the other, and felt a stabbing pain in the lower left side of his back. The pain surprised him. How long had it been? Almost a week without any bad pain at all.

Lucille looked at him closely, deep concern, compassion etched on her face. "Fergy? You all right, honey?"

He had to let the pain pass, trickle away in little spasms before answering.

"It is bad, baby?" she asked gently.

"It's goin' away," he mumbled, relief creeping across his face as the spasms stopped. He gulped the water and pills in two quick motions, handed her the glass and settled back slowly, carefully.

Lucille sat on the side of the bed. "Fergy?"

"Yeah, baby . . ." he answered, patting her thigh, trying to lighten the moment.

"What did the doctor say?"

"What did he say? Ooohh same-o same-o, keep on takin' your medicine, keep a lotta heat on and come back next

33

Monday."

"Did he   did he think you was gettin' any better?"

Fergy looked off, evasively, tempted to lie, but decided not to . . . Lucille was like radar on lies. "Uhh, well, lemme put it this way, baby   he said that he couldn't tell me that I was gettin' better or worse . . . With the kind o' thang I got, at my age, it could last for a long time or go away just like that!"

They were both silent for a few long moments, their thoughts blocking out the noises from the apartment next door, the rumbling of the el train a few blocks away and the heavy, wobbly sounds of someone stumbling through the hallway.

Lucille, coming back from the doldrums first, kicked her shoes off and began to prepare for bed. "Well, I was just wonderin'," she said absently.

He watched her unbutton her blouse, slip out of her skirt. Damn . . . how long had it been? Funny about my back, he thought, lacing his hands behind his head, some days I don't feel a thing and then, for no reason at all, making the slightest move, it feels like somebody had hit me in the back with an axe, or a sledgehammer.

Lucille smiled warmly at him and eased into the bathroom.

Sho' is a good woman . . . got to be a good woman to be goin' through all the shit she's been goin' through with me for the last eight months.

"Fergy, won't you be gettin' your check tomorrow?" she asked from the bathroom, the toilet gurgling erratically in the background.

" 'Sposed to," he answered evenly, "either I get it or I'm gon' have to go down there 'n cuss that dumb bitch out again."

Lucille giggled, Fergy flashed a broad smile at the ceiling, listening to her giggle   good to hear that sound for a change. Mrs. Swartz, the state workers' compensation rep-

34

resentative was a serious, standing joke between them. She was responsible for getting his monthly check out to him, but for some reason, she never seemed to be able to do it right two months in a row. God and Mrs. Swartz.

His smile faded, reconsidering the serious position she put them in, whenever she goofed. You could almost laugh about it, if you didn't feel like crying, he thought bitterly.

"How're things goin' with you 'n Mizz Bernhammer?" he asked, calculating the stages of Lucille's preparation for bed. Brushing her teeth now.

"Awwww, you know how it is, some days is better than others," she spat toothpaste into the toilet bowl, flushed it and re-entered the bedroom, blue middle-length negligee swirling about her thighs. Fergy's eyes danced from her breasts to her thighs and back, his eyelids hooded. "You know, I just walk 'round that woman's house sometimes, lookin' at all the advantages she has. Damned near everything in the house is automatic, 'cept me," she laughed sarcastically, sat down at her dressing table and started creaming her face.

"Can you imagine someone havin' all they bills paid? damned near nothing to do, really   but shop all day, and when she ain't doin' that she's drinkin'. Come to think of it, she's been drinkin' a long time now, but I didn't pay it too much attention 'til here lately.

"She came up to me today, breath smellin' like a distillery and started talkin' . . . Mrs. Smith, she says, yes, Mrs. Bernhammer . . . hate that name!   what can I do for you? I'm right in the middle of polishin' the silver, so you know damn well I ain't feelin' too much like no chitchat.

" 'Mrs. Smith, how long have you worked for me?'

"How long? Five 'n a half years, I told her, on my guard all the way, you know? 'cause ain't no tellin' what gits in middle-aged white women's heads sometimes. Anyway, she looks down in her gin glass for awhile and finally looks up

35

into my face and says, slurs would be a better way to put it, almost with tears in her eyes, 'Mrs. Smith, why can't we be friends?'

"For a second I had the urge to jab one of those forks I was polishing in her eye, but then I thought, nawww, don't do that, Lucille   she's just drunk, and besides she ain't even worth killin'.

"I stopped polishin' the silver and asked her, 'Mrs. Bernhammer, how in the hell we gon' be friends while I'm sittin' up here, polishin' a bunch o' knives 'n forks 'n spoons o' yours, that you don't even use but once a month? In addition to that, you ain't payin' me enough for us to be friends.'

"She walked away, behind that, sobbin' in her drink. Yeahh, white folks is sho' nuff hard to figure out sometimes, I think it's rainin'.'"

She stood at the wall switch, looking at his peaceful expres-

She stood up and faced the bed, and Fergy's angelic dreamless expression. She crossed over to him on tiptoe and kissed his forehead. Poor baby, bet he'll be glad when he stops takin' those pills, they knock him out faster than a cat can lick his ass.

She stood at the wall switch, looking at his peaceful expression, and measured the distance she'd have to cover in the dark after flicking the light off, smiled as she glided to bed in the dark, remembering all the times Fergy had stubbed his toe against the bedstead or a chair on his way to bed.

"Goodnight, baby," she whispered into his sleeping ears and turned her back to him, her arms aching from the wax job she had given the Bernhammer living room that afternoon.

God, I hope I ain't coming down with bursitis or something   that'd be all we'd need.

Kanoon Al-Haddi, once known before his conversion to Islam

36

as Milfred Hawkins, stood center stage, bathed in a luminous spotlight, his precious bassoon perched on a stand next to him, playing an African thumb piano solo. The Pot's Monday night jazz audience, a confection of semi-professional musicians, professional musicians, deep believers, cool dudes and their ladies, sat mesmerized by Kanoon's passionate involvement with his art.

During the course of the playing of one particularly tricky phrase, Kanoon looked out at the audience, tears forming in his eyes, lips trembling, and moaned.

"Git down, Kanoon! git on down to stone soul!" a high Gemini lady, unable to bear the tension any longer, called out to him.

Flicking into and through the phrase again, satisfied that he was getting exactly what he wanted, he slid away from it and signalled, with an arrogant turn of his head, for the re-entrance of his quintet.

The quintet's sound, Mediterranean-Afro-Cuban-New World African, danced past his staccato piano playing, the little box held up close to the microphone now, wobbled back artfully to the last phrase he had played and slithered to an end.

The audience stood as one and applauded wildly.

Kanoon bowed, ever so slightly, a cold smile flickering at the corners of his mouth. Good, really good, he thought, to see the people giving themselves up to Another Music.

He nodded solemnly to the members of his group, taking the measure of each one as he did so. Armandito on congas, a fiercely proud little black dervish from Matanzas, Cuba, who acted and played as though rhythm belonged to him. Sheikh Baby on oud, Buford Knobbs singing on every sized flute currently known, doubling on chekere and double gong; Pablo Cruz-Extrana playing the cello with so much quickness and grace that people were always asking why the dude

37

was playing this oversized guitar, standing on end like that. Them, that is, who weren't hip to the fact that Cruz-Extrana was a genius. Baby Blood blew soprano sax and loved ragaic solos, always seemed to be mad at somebody or something, but showed none of that kind of feeling as he spooled out yard after yard of brutally honest song.

"Concerto for Bassoon!" someone yelled.

"Yeahhh! Concerto for Bassoon!" somebody else picked up the request.

He stood at the edge of the stage and let them come at him in full voice before he took a backward step to his instrument.

"Yeahhh, gon' put the pot on!"

"Con-certo for Bassoooooon, Ka-nooooooon!"

"Right on, brother!"

He picked his bassoon up from its stand, glared the audience into submissive silence, . . . paused to deep-breathe several times, to tune in with the members of his group, and gestured the music into being   "Uh one! uhh two! uh three!"

Cruz-Extrana loved the Concerto for Bassoon, and it showed in his method of attack. A so-called jazz critic, unable to get past Pablo's long black eyelashes and his slender, delicately tapered fingers, called his opening statement, the Chinese Blues. Pablo and Kanoon had laughed themselves to tears reading the review. It was obvious that the reviewer had never heard of a saeta, nor had he ever heard La Nina de los Peines or Manitas de Plata's cousin, Jose Reyes, sing one.

He slipped Baby Blood in behind the cello's opening statement, nodding warmly at the Baby's deep, searching, slurry sounds. Buford trailed in, swiping at the Baby's tail ends with little melodic swoops and whoops, Sheikh Baby counterpointed with his oud, Armandito calmly put the chekere aside and got down on his congas with a rhythmic pattern that was

38

almost Hindu Indian in its complexity.

The unit, jellied into place with the first movement, slowed down to pick Kanoon up in the second section and stretched out from there.

Kanoon, never content to feel his way up and down old scales, frowned at the familiarity of his first notes, erased the memory of them with a succession of finely woven statements, profound commentaries on his state of mind and the deep regard he had for beauty and the truth that his instrument was capable of exploring. The Gemini lady's eyes glistened, and the corners of her mouth grew moist as she listened, each of his notes a precious piece of advice to her consciousness.

Kanoon fixed her mind with a soulful glance at the end of the piece, and told her, in eye language, that he wanted her to follow him back to his dressing room at the conclusion of the set.

The audience, satisfied with another reading of his trademark work, the avant garde of Another Music, allowed him to leave the stage, opening up an aisle of adoration to his dressing room.

The Gemini lady, a lyrically constructed, Ethiopian looking cocainist, her head held high, followed him, dazzled by the idea that she was going to be given the privilege of serving the master. Warm applause and many jealous looks followed them as they turned the far corner of the club, another kind of creativity about to happen.

Fred Lee nudged Bessie gently, "That's it, baby . . . you'll be lucky if you see Mil   uhh   Kanoon, again 'til Friday. We better git on outta here so I can get up tomorrow."

Bessie laughed out loud, a fine gin 'n Squirt film clouding her vision, good vibes and her man cooling out all negatives. They made their way through the crowd, portions of it milling around as though they had been led astray, while others

39

sat, patiently waiting, hoping that Kanoon, after the "girl" and the woman, would return for another set.

It was never possible to know what was going to happen in the Pot, mainly because the place belonged to Kanoon, or possibly, as rumor had it, to one of his numerous ladyfriends. It was said that Kanoon, weeks after his opening, got onstage one night and explained, in no uncertain terms, what the policy of the Pot was going to be. The versions varied with the people telling the story, but it was generally agreed that he had said that the Pot would be on from Monday to Saturday, that it might only be simmering sometimes, to allow the amateur cooks a chance with their unorthodox recipes

but, for the most part, they would be cookin'! ... everything that was musically edible.

Bessie and Fred Lee struggled into their coats in the crowded foyer of the club and then eased out into the cold night. Bessie held Fred Lee's arm, fending off competition with the move, admiring her man's wide-brimmed, silver crowned hat, his full, beaver brush mustache and the peacockish way he carried imself.

He broke into laughter as they walked.

"What's funny, baby?" she asked him, already smiling, the contagion spreading.

"I was   hahhhahhahhh   I was thinkin' about one night, remember? one night at the Pot when Kanoon came onstage, sat down and started readin' the newspaper."

Bessie's laughter echoed his, "Yeahhh! yeahhh! I remember that!"

"What was it he said when people got pissed off and started fat mouthin' 'im?!"

"Well, aside from callin' the people in the audience a bunch o' stupid motherfuckers and tin-eared baboons and a bunch o' other ol' weird-ass things   he said ... he said ...."

"Oh, I remember   if Beethoven was up here, you

40

wouldn't be askin' him to perform on cue, like a fuckin' trained seal or somethin', so why should I? or somethin' like that, and walked off the stage."

Bessie shook her head, "Kanoon is crazy as hell."

"Really!" Fred Lee agreed, "but that motherfucker be playin' a whole lotta music."

Fred Lee slowed his step, thoughtfully checking out the dark areas on the street ahead of him, alert for midnight fliers, delinquents and the pigs. "Uhh," he continued, satisfied that the way was safe, "uhh, yeah, yeah, I guess you could say he was crazy, in a way. But dig what the dude done did. First thing he did, which was really superslick, right after he made a lil' bread off his first few albums, was to buy a club, right in the neighborhood."

"Well, you know what they say 'bout that, 'bout who got the club for him?"

"Uhh huh, yeah, well, that may be true. But the fact remains, the dude got a place to play his own music, I mean, like he can git funky as a motherfucker up in the Pot and ain't got to answer to nobody   No-body!"

"I hadn't really thought about it like that."

"Yeah, dig it! I was standin' 'round, me 'n Jake the Fake."

"You 'n who?" Bessie eyed him suspiciously.

Fred Lee smiled and lowered his hand to pat her affectionately on the rump.

"I said me 'n Jake the Fake, baby   but don't be gettin' all excited 'n shit. I ran into him one evenin' and we stopped for a taste in the Pot. No, baby   no deals, no schemes, we just stopped for a taste, to rap a lil' while.

"Anyway, Kanoon was talkin' to a bunch o' dudes at the bar, tellin' them that he represented the New Breed, that he was one o' them new niggers that didn't have to give the white boy shit, didn't have to play what they wanted him to play, didn't have to pay them no rent, and wasn't waitin' 'round

41

hopin' that they would decide to recognize his black ass, he was doin' his own thang, and them what didn't like it could kiss his ass, the red, inner meat part of it."

"Well, I'll say!" Bessie exclaimed as they strolled on, pride in her man bubbling her up like a pigeon. She peeked at him out of the corner of her eye. Was that stuff Miss Rabbit gave me to use, after he got out of the joint, really responsible for him being the way he is now? Or what?

"Why you lookin' at me outta the corner of your eyes like that, woman?" he asked, a humorous glint in his own eyes.

" 'Cause I love you, Fred Lee, that's why."

He squeezed her waist, slimmer now by twenty pounds since she'd gone on a strict diet. "C'mon, we got a block to go, you used to be pretty fast, I'll race you to the front steps."

Bessie bent over, snatched her shoes off and struck out, giggling like a teenager before Fred Lee realized she had put forty yards between them.

He eased into a sprinter's stride after a few yards, the years of doing wind sprints in the prison yard showing up in every smooth movement. Yeahhh suhh, it was sho' 'nuff lookin' good, he thought, as he breezed past Bessie with a grin. Woman lookin' good, I'm lookin' good, only thing wrong is this jive job I got   gotta do better than this mail-clerk messenger bullshit   gotta do somethin' else.

He dashed to the top step of the porch fronting their apartment building, barely breathing hard, and watched Bessie pause at the bottom, exhausted.

"You cheated, Fred Lee!" she accused him, mounting the steps.

"How in the hell could I cheat when you started out first?"

"You just did!" she responded with impeccable logic and eased past him, glowing from the run, feeling giddy.

He followed her up the dimly lit stairs, carefully checking

out the dimples in the back of her legs and her lately found, hourglass figure.

Yeahhh, thangs was definitely lookin' up.

Chapter 2
Getting There

Sweet Peter Deeder, now known by his given name, Peter Dawson, but still better known by the regulars as Sweet Peter Deeder, ex-pimp, ex-dope peddler, ex-gambling house owner, ex-conman, ex-ex . . . calmly shuffled his pages of notes, sitting onstage at St. Anastasia's College for Girls. He stared up through the slitted Gothic windows at the clear, bright autumn sky. Tuesday weather, an ol' con buddy once called it.

He glanced down at the first row of multicolored, fleshy teenaged knees, catching sight of a thigh crossed over a thigh, the taut young meat straining under its short, pleated covering . . . and sighed. God! he asked himself, directing his eyes back up through the slits, God! what the hell am I doin' up in here?

Very simple, his mercilessly logical side spoke to him, you

45

gittin' over, motherfucker! gittin' over like a fat rat!

The assembly hall filled, the fresh, sparkling complexions of the school girls glowed, the pledge to the flag was listlessly recited and the Mother Superior introduced Mr. Peter Dawson, lecturer on Sinfulness.

Sweet Peter D. limped over to the lectern, hip mod garments cloaking his slight paunch, a dazzling silk scarf covering the grillwork of scar tissue on the left side of his neck, a memo from Kwendi and company, from years ago, that and the ankle that never healed right.

He stood as straight as a tin soldier for a few beats, taking the measure of his audience and allowing them the same liberty. For a moment, the hot flash of the urge to pimp again made him shudder, the mad feeling of wanting to fly out into the middle of this audience of seventeen, eighteen and nineteen year old cunts, to spool off yards of honey language, of lovestick and knuckle sandwiches, to crack their innocent young skulls open with an Arabian Nights tale of the glories to be found in whoring for him.

The lights in the hall seemed to dim as he leaned forward, the theatrical effect created by a passing cloud, and said in a super mellow tone of voice, "Today, young ladies   I would like to talk to you about the second oldest profession, pimpin'," and then added, almost as an afterthought, "and the dangers and evils of the first oldest profession, whorin'."

He leaned back, pausing for effect, and roamed his catchin' eye up and down the first row.

His eyes took them in three times around, involuntarily, the first three at the end. A black black girl with sacrilegious breasts spitting up at him through a tense blouse like twin cobras, a Mongolian princess next to her, her cheeks all flat planes with slittled goggles for eyes, slouched down so far in her seat that the school's pleated uniform skirt fell between her strong yellow thighs like gauze. And next to her; Sweet

46

Peter caught himself, sucked in a little air for strength, next to her was a cornstalked monster of a blonde with a lush rose bow mouth and creamy thighs that started under her armpits and almost stretched across the division of space between the first row and the stage apron.

He shook his head sadly, as though lamenting the evils of pimpin' 'n whorin'. smiled accidentally at the crusted face of the Mother Superior seated onstage to his left, and turned back to face the eight-hundred and forty-six challenges to his self control.

"Yes, today . . . young ladies, I'm goin' to talk to you about two of the world's worst professions. I speak to you as an ex-member of one of those professions, I leave it up to your imaginations to guess which one I was into."

He felt a slight dampness swell under his armpit as the Mongolian princess, an overgrown Lolita, holding eyeball to eyeball contact with him, gently scratched her crotch.

I'm gon' have to tell my goddamned agent not to be bookin' me into no more girls' schools, he mumbled subconsciously as he bent to pick up his fumbled notes.

Mr. Chickens, his four super-obedient hens delicately high-stepping around him and his ace, the Spinning Top Dude, stood under the lengthening shadow of a fire escape, just around an alley corner's edge, trying to defeat the autumn evening's chill with a pint of cheap pluck.

They said nothing to each other as they passed the bottle back and forth, ignoring the people who passed, glancing at the two of them with a variety of attitudes. The Spinning Top Dude killed the corner and stooped quickly to set the empty bottle down behind him as the squad car turned the corner of the alley.

"One dime, one show!" Mr. Chickens sang out, hip to the ways to gain the upper hand over the police mentality. "One dime one show!" he called out again, a note of urgency in his gravelly voice, and began to cluck to his chickens, to line them up at the side of the alley.

The Spinning Top Dude, a master of the string and hourglass top, or the spherical top or any other kind of top that would slide up a string, a wizened brown man with soft almond shaped eyes, thirty-eight years away from Luzon, in the Philippines, had already uncorked his works and had three hourglass forms doing figure eights in mid-air, handling them almost telepathically as he hummed a quiet little tune in Tagalog the whole time.

"One dime, one show!" Mr. Chickens almost screamed into the squad car's window, clucking furiously out of the corner of his mouth for his chickens to roll over in unison. Mr. Chickens and the Spinning Top Dude performed with an air of desperation around the fringes of their movements, doing anything not to be hauled in on a vagrancy pop. Both of them, having had it happen before, knew the dangers of incarceration.

For Mr. Chickens, it meant that his precious chickens would be disposed of in somebody's skillet,   the Spinning Top Dude's tops confiscated, their art lost.

The Spinning Top Dude hummed louder, paraded his three sandalwood carvings through an intricate cat's cradle behind his back, while Mr. Chickens half-stepped through a rhumba with his hens.

The two pigs, one black and the other white, looked at them contemptuously from the warmth of their squad car. The black one sarcastically tossed a half-dollar at Mr. Chicken's feet, "Lets see that fucked up tightrope thing you guys do."

With an athletic movement, surprising to see in someone Mr. Chickens' age, he scooped the half-dollar up, slipped it under the layers of his coats, sweaters and shirts, into his watch fob pocket and turned to the Spinning Top Dude without a word.

Their movements synchronized, the Spinning Top Dude popped the last top off of the string and into his side pocket, held the end of the string out to Mr. Chickens as they both knelt on the cold pavement of the alley.

Mr. Chickens flicked a few corn chips out of one of his many pockets to his ladies, clucked them lovingly onto the lowered tightrope one by one, and pulled it taut as they scrambled across, wings flapping, bills opened for balance.

The Spinning Top Dude spooled a cylindrical top onto the string behind the last highwire hen and, with the finesse of hundreds of hours of practice, popped the top high into the air as he, Mr. Chickens and the hens made a deep bow to their snobbish audience, catching it on the string behind his back, almost as an afterthought, seconds later.

The two creatures in the car threw their heads back, laughing uncontrollably for a few carefree moments, at the sight of the two pathetic figures, a dirty brick wall with obscene scrawlings on it their backdrop, a pile of smelly garbage to the left and right of them.

The white pig, still red in the face from laughing so hard in his tight collar, leaned across his partner to say, as they slowly pulled away, "Awright, that's enough of that bullshit for today, you bums clear this alley, next time we catch you two loitering we're gonna run ya in!"

The black one nodded in agreement, still smiling.

Mr. Chickens removed his scarecrow's hat, revealing a mass of tattered, Shirley Temple forelocks, and bowed graciously the Spinning Top Dude created the momentary illusion of a top spinning through his head by whipping the string around his head five times. They watched the car reach the end of the alley in respectful silence.

"Goddamn mother-fuckers!" the Spinning Top Dude muttered fiercely.

49

Mr. Chickens dismissed the hostility with a smiling, "Fuck them! they ain't shit!" and held up the shiny half-dollar "C'mon, Tops, le's go git another short dog."

The Spinning Top Dude and Mr. Chickens shuffled out of the alley, stumbling against each other for support, on their way to the corner liquor store, trailed by four dirty, funky chickens, stepping abreast.

The neighborhood, returning from their eight-hour spirit drainage sessions on the plantations about town, smiled fondly at the sight.

The Holt family, minus son number one, Perry, off on a date with his bride to be, sat around the card table-dinner table in the front room, looking at an eight by ten photograph of a two-story house. Nathan Holt, at fifty-one, rangy and lean, passed the picture back to his wife, Diane   a sour look pulling the corners of his mouth down.

Mrs. Holt placed the photo between her and her youngest son, rubbed shoulders with him excitedly. "Isn't it just lovely, Byron?" she asked him, her eyes shining.

"Yeahhh, it's really outta sight, Momma."

Nathan leaned back in his chair and lit an after-dinner cigarette, a heavier scowl crinkling his mouth, looking at his woman and son admire their prospective home.

"I sure wish Perry was here," he grumbled.

"Why, Daddy?" Byron asked in a very respectful voice.

"Well," he directed his answer to his wife, "he's gon' be livin' in this place too, so I don't see why we couldn't all sit down like folks and decide what we was goin' to do, together."

Diane, slightly exasperated, pursed her lips. "Now Nathan, we've been over this fifty times in the last two months. Perry has already told us he's gettin' married and that he won't be livin' with us, so I don't think what he would have to say would be too important, one way or the other."

50

Nathan mumbled into his mustache and blew a thick patch of smoke across the table.

Mother and son exchanged meaningful glances.

"Nathan, we've got to get this straightened out right here 'n now, for all time. We have a home paid down on, we've made all the legal arrangements and everything . . . Now just tell me, do you or don't you want to move out of this lousy ass neighborhood and into this nice home out south, or not? Which is it, damnit?!"

Father and son both reacted, slightly shocked to hear the lady of the house use profanity, an unusual act for her.

"Awwww bay-beee," Nathan began, trying to cool her out.

"Don't awwww bay-beee me, Nathan Holt! We've been up 'n down, in 'n out about this thing, and all you come up with is negative vibes, now let's get it ironed out now, once 'n for all!"

Nathan straightened up a little, determined not to be bullied. "Ahhemmm, Byron, leave us in here for a lil' while, me and your mother have some important business to discuss."

Byron, Momma's boy, nineteen years old and feeling older, bristled slightly at his father for the second time in his life, confident that his mother was going to back him up. "Why should I have to leave? This concerns me just as much as it does anybody. I mean, like, after all, I'm still livin' at home, and I'm gon' be helpin' to make the payments 'n everything."

Diane Holt shot protective words between them quickly, preventing Nathan from heaving the table onto Byron's rebellious head. "He's right, Nathan! right! right down to the bone! This concerns the three of us more than anybody me, you and Byron, he's right! Whatever you and I have to say should be said, right here 'n now, in front of By'," she concluded, patting Byron's shoulder protectively.

Nathan Holt, his eyes squinched half shut with anger,

slowly relaxed, seeing, despite his urge to kick Byron's ass, the validity of her statement.

"Awright! awright! I'll say what I got to say. Number one, I told you a long time ago, Diane, that I didn't give a mule's fart for the idea of ownin' no house, nowheres, bein' stuck for no twenty year mortage ..."

She interrupted, bearing down, "Yeah, uhhn huh, that's true! but you did agree, if I remember correctly, that it wasn't makin' too much sense to keep on payin' the kind o' money for rent that we've been payin' for the last twelve years."

"With all the rats 'n roaches," Byron added helpfully.

"Number two, if you all will kindly let me go on?" he continued sarcastically. "Number two, I was against the idea of movin' way out south where this place is, with all them ol' saddidy niggers 'cause ..."

Diane, on top of his semi-arguments unmercifully, "Yes, Nathan, you *were* against the idea of movin' out south, at first   but then you rejected the northside 'cause you said you didn't know anybody over there. You said you didn't like the westside because of what you called 'all them crazy ass Miss'ssippi niggers runnin' 'round with switchblades.'

"We don't have anything but the lake to the east of us, so actually it was your idea, to begin with, to move out south, if we were goin' to buy property anywhere."

"She's right, Daddy," Byron added solemnly, feeling more heroic with every moment that passed without his father attacking him.

Nathan Holt stubbed out the fag-end of his cigarette, lit another one and stared out of their front room window, pissed off. The el train, passing by a couple blocks away, shot past his view and gave the apartment its customary tremor. The squalling of a police siren, shotgun blasts, or the backfire from someone's car, coupled to an obscene argument being had on the sidewalk below their window filtered up to their

52

ears during Father Holt's silent interim.

"Well?" he asked finally. "Whatchall want me t' say?"

"Tell Momma you dig the idea of us ownin' a pad of our own, Daddy!" Byron blurted out, an earnest look on his thin, sensitive face.

Mrs. Holt waved away the suggestion with a fluttered movement of her hands, her head lowered sadly. "No, no . . . By', don't ask your father to do no such thing . . ." She paused, as though searching for something to say that she couldn't find the words for, heavy old woman's lines suddenly etched in her face.

"You know something?" she continued thoughtfully, speaking to no one in particular. "Just about all my life I've had someone accuse me of wantin' more than they thought I was entitled to. When I was young, down home, with my light skin and what they used to call 'good hair,' colored folks was on my case 'cause they thought I was tryin' to be white, while the peckerwoods called me an uppidy nigger wench who was always fulla sass . . . ."

"Diane!?"

She ignored her husband's attempted interruption, speaking through it as though she were in a trance. "Then, later on, after we moved up north and I had a chance to go to a junior college for almost two years, I had people tell me that it didn't make sense for a black girl to be wastin' time in school 'cause all I was gonna do was get married 'n have babies anyway . . . ."

"Momma?"

"I resented that for a long time, that is, 'til I got married, got lucky would be a better way to put it, and had a couple beautiful sons . . . ."

The apartment had developed an eerie look, lit in the front room by the flickering neon lights from outside, from within from the kitchen light shining through the hallway.

53

"Nathan?" she veered off at him suddenly.

"Yeah, baby," he responded in a low voice.

"You remember what it was like for us when we first got married, how hard things were right after the Depression?"

Nathan nodded, his face a glacial African mask in the dim light.

She looked at Byron warmly, mother's memories swelling her mind. "Raising two screamin', hungry   at one point, I thought Perry was gonna eat me alive. People were havin' it harder than they'd ever had it, but we kept right on pushin'   yes indeed, we kept right on pushin'."

Byron folded his arms and leaned on the table, staring at his mother reverently.

She reached across the table and placed her hand on top of her man's big work-veined paw. "We kept right on pushin' because I have a man who has never let me down."

Nathan patted her hand, stroked it on top of his, warmly.

She spoke directly to Byron, "He's made fun of me, from time to time, about listenin' to classical music, white folks' music, and going to art shows or doin' a few other things that we don't see eye to eye on, but," and here she turned back to her husband, "he's never let me down. Now, after we've gone through all the trials 'n tribulations to make ends meet, fought with your folks and mine ... yours, 'cause they didn't think I was good enough for you, and mine 'cause they thought I was too good for you ... after we've gone through all that, in addition to raisin' two wonderful sons in the middle of all this."

She swept her hands out to embrace the grimy apartment, shaking slightly again from another train, the wandering roach trekking up the wall behind her and the hip rats patiently waiting for them to split so that they could check out the scene for leftovers.

"Don't worry, baby," Nathan reassured her grimly, before

54

she could go on, "I'm not gon' let you down this time either. When're those people movin' out of our house?"

Byron resisted the urge to go around the corner of the table and kiss his father, knowing he would never understand.

Mother Holt, taking it all in stride, replied, easing away from the table with their dessert saucers, "Next week. We can start packin' Friday."

Byron followed his mother from the table into the kitchen, gave her a peck on the cheek and moved on to his room, George Cain's *Blueschild Baby* waiting to be read. Nathan Holt sat in the darkened front room thinking evil thoughts.

Bet the goddamned President would be happy as a pigeon with a perch on city hall to see me settin' here in the dark, with his save-the-energy bullshit.

"Nathan! I'm goin' to bed, you comin'?" his love called from the kitchen seductively.

"In a few minutes, honey," he called back, his baritone huskier than usual, and lit another cigarette. Why in the world should I *not* be wantin' to move to a more decent place? he questioned himself as another train rumbled past. He sat smoking, fighting with the question, rejecting all of his old objections one by one. Friends? Shit! I can see them on the weekend. Or whenever. Being farther away from work? Transportation was better out south, and you wouldn't have to fight a bunch of young gangsters with no respect for their elders for a seat   Well, not all the time anyway.

And what was really wrong about owning somethin' of your own anyway? Even if it did take twenty years?

Perry popped in, eyes shining and pants front stiff from a half hour of declared love and wonderful promises.

"Heyyy, Dad, what's happenin'?" he asked in his usual flighty manner. "Why you sittin' up here in the dark, fuses blown again?"

Nathan Holt stubbed his cigarette out and strolled past his

55

number one son growling, "Where were you when I needed you, boy?"

Perry followed his departure through the narrow hallway leading to his parents' bedroom, extremely puzzled by his old man's morose question.

Wowwww   wonder what that was all about?   Oh well,   wonder if Momma left me somethin' in the stove?

Lubertha tiptoed through the short hallway, heading for her room.

"Lubertha!" her father's gruff voice stopped her, caused her to roll her eyes to the ceiling in exasperation.

"Yes, Daddy?"

He leaned around the corner separating the hallway from the kitchen, in his tattered, plaid, horse collar, terry cloth robe. "C'mon on in here 'n have a beer with me," he said to her, the invitation sounding more like an order.

She slouched through the hallway, tired from a full day's work and four hours of Club business. She sat across the kitchen table from her father, watching him pop the top on two beers. She smiled her thanks at him as he pushed the can out to her with gruff grace.

Fathers are really funny, she thought, looking over the edge of her can at her own. The beer ritual, for example, had started exactly on her twenty-first birthday   Prior to that she had received every threat that an authoritarian like Ed Franklin could hand out on the subject of intoxicants of all kinds. Since that time they had been into a jug of Jack together a few times.

"You up pretty late, ain't you, Daddy?"

He belched twice and stroked the suds from his walrus mustache, filled with gray hair, Lubertha noticed, a little surprised at the sight. "Couldn't sleep," he answered in his usual, laconic fashion. They matched sips a few times, each wait-

56

ing for the other one to lead.

She watched him spin his beer can around slowly in the wet ring it had made on the table, knowing that he wanted to rap, but that his basically conservative nature wouldn't allow it to happen, not right off, anyway.

"How's Kwendi?" he asked, leading off finally.

The thought slipped through her head before she answered

That's really sweet, ol' man   really sweet of you to ask that.

"He's doin' o.k. I got a long letter from him Friday."

Ed Franklin tensed his jaw muscles and took a long dip. "You know somethin'? I been doin' a lil' thinkin' about that conversation we had the other night . . . ."

Lubertha stifled a full-fledged grin, knowing that he would have had to do more than just a "lil' thinkin' " on the subjects they had tripped through a six pack on.

"First off, I'm gon' say this, I ain't never been 'shamed to admit when I was wrong."

"What were you wrong about, Daddy?" she asked sweetly.

"Well, a couple thangs," he admitted cautiously, getting another brew from the box   "You want another one o' these?"

She quickly drained her can and nodded yes. It looked suspiciously like a three can discussion brewing. A bit of her weariness dissolved with the prospect of rappin' with her ol' man.

"O.k., now then," he continued, "I still don't go 'long with all the funny styled ideas you and Kwendi and y'all's bunch believe in, but I go 'long with what you was sayin' 'bout the political parties . . . there really ain't too daggoned much difference between the Democrats 'n the Republicans . . . ."

"What made you reach that conclusion?"

"Well," he searched for the right answer for a few seconds, "hell, I been studyin' 'em all my life."

57

"But what made you come to that conclusion?" she persisted.

"Let's just say I been studyin' 'em but I hadn't been thinkin' about 'em."

They smiled at each other and took unison sips.

"But anyway," he went on, lowering the can, "even if there ain't too much difference 'tween 'em, we still need 'em."

Ohhh ohhh, here we go, Lubertha thought, knowing that he was egging her into one of their pet discussions, one that she was forcing him to pay more and more attention to all the time. She placed her can on the table and leaned toward him, the cords in her throat pulsing out.

"Daddy, you know that ain't true."

"What ain't true?"

"That we need the present system."

"That's not what I said, I said we need the political parties we got, even if ain't too much difference 'tween 'em."

"That's what I'm talkin' about, the Democrats and the Republicans represent the present system, and the present system stinks." The words snapped out with a little more force than she had intended, causing her father to stare at her for a hard five seconds. "O.k.," she continued, a bit more mildly, "let me put it this way, for a few hundred years now, the people who run this country,   the rich people, meanin' the white folks, have tried to convince all the rest of us that all we had to do, in order to change things was to vote for the Republicans if you didn't like the way things were goin', or the Democrats, whichever one was in power at the moment."

"I been a Democrat for twenny years," Father Franklin shot in, not exactly delighted to hear his daughter run down the America he had voted for.

"But," Lubertha continued earnestly, "what they didn't tell us, the lil' po' dumb believers, is that the money people run

58

both parties, and when it gets to a point of makin' a decision about whether we're goin' to have good government or dirty money, it'll be dirty money every time."

Ed Franklin fished a pack of cigarettes out of his robe pocket, lit up and looked at Lubertha with a deep frown.

"Hold on now, you done lost me somewhere . . . and I don't mean about the money part; I know, for a fact that all them slimy politicians got they hands in the kitty   but I'm still sayin' that this system is still the best."

Lubertha rode past her father, knowing that she would get bogged down if she allowed him to deviate too much. "Daddy, let's just stay with the money part for a minute   'cause that's really what it's all about. Those names they've stuck on these so-called political parties don't really count. For all we know, a couple billionaires in Argentina or somewhere may have gotten together with a couple billionaires in the U.S. of A. to decide who was gonna be president for the next four years, or vice versa . . . ."

"Ain't you forgettin' somethin'?" he asked sarcastically, certain that he had a nail for her.

"What's that?"

"What about the people? You forget, we vote whoever we want into office   even in Miss'ssippi nowadays."

Lubertha gulped her beer and almost choked on it in her hurry to reply. "I disagree, Daddy. We *think* we vote whoever we want into office. In this day 'n age, television, meanin' Big Money, makes the vote happen for whoever Big Money is behind."

Ed Franklin smiled at his daughter's logic, liking and disliking her opposition. "Hmf! Sho' is cold, daughter. Sho' is cold. To let you tell it, the American voter ain't got a leg to stand on."

"It may sound cold, but facts are colder still. If the American voter had a leg to stand on, things wouldn't be in

59

the messed up shape they're in now."

He shook his head slowly, picked up his can and drained it, thinking hard. "Awright, things ain't as good as they could be, but we still got it better than most other folks in the world."

"The reason why," she answered promptly, "is because we've no, no, I can't say *we*, lets say *they've* exploited, cheated, conned, warred and ripped off all the rest of the world for as long as they've been in power, the only things we've received have been the leftovers, the crumbs from the ripoffs and you can bet your bottom dollar that if they had a way of keeping the crumbs away from us, they would've done it a long time ago."

"These billionaires you talkin' about?"

"Uh huh, one 'n the same, some of 'em have English names, Spanish, Greek, Indian, German, Arabic, Jewish a lot of 'em have Japanese names these days. The point is, when they link up to exploit, their names are all the same, Exploitation."

Ed Franklin shrugged away the wild urge to snatch his daughter across the table, pull her across his knees and spank her. "Awright! awright! money rules! the rich run every damned thing and all the rest of us fools is just runnin' 'round tryin' to survive. Awright! I'll go for it. Now lemme ask you this, since you seem to have all the answers. What other way could thangs be? And how you gonna get 'em that way?"

Lubertha shook the dregs of her can down her throat, a warm, deliberate calm settling over her. What other way, and how? "Let me put it a couple ways, Daddy. Number one, I think we ought to change the jive political system that doesn't guarantee the best standard of life possible for all the people."

"Nawww, no m'am, you ain't gon' take me all over the world, I'm just dealin' with the U-nited States, let's just stay up in here for awhile."

She listened to his slight slurring carefully, aware that she

60

would have to be a little more diplomatic now, knowing from past experience how easily his aggression was set off by her theories.

"O.k., just in America, hugh?"

"Thasss right, just in America!"

"Well," she started in again, the brew and her thoughts swirling around, "I don't wanna get placed in a position of havin' to say that this should be done before that, or vice versa ."

Ed Franklin, up to pull the last two brews out of the box, spoke over his shoulder. "I don't give a damn what order you put 'em in, just lay it out for me. You always talkin' 'bout changes 'n revolutions 'n whatnot, well, here's your chance! Run it out for me."

Lubertha accepted another can, took a deep sip. "Well, to begin with, the best thing we could do to start off with is to equalize things make certain that there were no outrageously rich people or outrageously poor people."

"Oh, you talkin' about communism then!" he announced smugly.

"No, not really," she answered, her mind wandering. "That's the trouble with how we get hung up between semantics and concepts. The concept of everybody havin' enough to eat, a decent place to stay and good clothes to wear doesn't mean communism. What I'm talkin' about has to do with the people being granted the human right to live like human beings, minus all the fake hustle and drummed up drama that the people who control things lay on us."

She paused for a long sip, into it now. "I mean, look at it this way, Daddy this country is too rich for anyone to be poor in it. It just doesn't make sense. Like, is it really necessary for some ol' dude to be livin' in a fifty room house, just because he manages to cheat somebody out of a million bucks a year?

61

"O.K., startin' with the wealth factor, spread that all the way out, that way you wouldn't have Big Money runnin' the political setup. It might mean that the best man could be found for the job of runnin' the country, or the county, or the city or whatever, rather than the one who has the most oil money behind him.

"I could stay for a long time on the money thing because that's what messes up a lot of other things here.

"But it's so tied in with the racism thang that you really can't separate the two. The white people who run this place, the altogether racists, not the All in the Family racists, have such a vested interest in institutional racism that they are even thinkin' of, if not actually callin' their own children niggers,

not in the sense that they called us niggers, but in a different kind of way, simply because their children don't want to be oppressors like their mothers 'n fathers have been."

Ed took a long pull on his beer, eyes shining, waiting for a mistake to happen that he could figure out.

"So, along with equalizin' things on the economic front, we should have a complete overthrow of the racial scheme of things, and I *ain't talkin'* about integration either. I think it would be stupid to try to legislate social habits. What we should have is a system that guarantees, absolutely *guarantees* the best woman or man the opportunity to do meaningful work, for a *living* wage; regardless of race.

"That would settle a bunch of problems, if we could solve the white racial problem. I know we can't solve it by killin' all the white folks."

Lubertha stopped, her heart pumping faster. "Kwendi says that we ought to put groups of the best so-called minority group minds in Think-Do-Tanks for a month, dealin' with each one of the problems we have here."

"Minority group minds?" Father Franklin asked, slightly worn down.

62

"Uh huh, his thing is that the so-called majority group mind, the white mind, has so completely messed itself around that it will never be straightened out enough to deal with the problems they've created. If they'd been able to, once again, things wouldn't be in the state they're in today."

"So, you sayin', you 'n Kwendi 'n him, that Negroes gon' solve the country's problems, huh?"

"Right on! Chicanos, Indians, Asians, Blacks, us!" Lubertha's intensity took her voice almost to the Club meeting level. Her father stared at her as though he were seeing his daughter for the first time.

Mrs. Franklin shuffled into the kitchen, yawning, wandered past them sitting at the table like a sleepwalker and poured herself a glass of water from the cold water jug in the refrigerator. "You two gon' sit up here boozin' 'n flappin' your jaws all night?" she asked, almost as an afterthought, as she shuffled back to bed.

Father and daughter burst into broad grins as they watched her shambling departure.

"Momma's got a point, we both gotta get up tomorrow."

"Yeahhh," Ed Franklin agreed sourly, crushing his beer can in his paw. "But we ain't got to the end o' this," he reminded his daughter.

"By no means!" she agreed, as she clicked off the kitchen light, the last one out, and headed wearily for her bedroom.

63

Chapter 3
Ways of Making Bread

Arnold C., for Charles Mack, but better known as "Chili" to the dudes he had played high school basketball with, sprawled out in his king-sized bed, scratching his crotch with his left hand and reaching for the half smoked joint in the swan-shaped ashtray bedside, a token of last night's doin's, with the other hand.

He lit the roach and took a deep hit. Wednesday, 12:15, what time was she supposed to show up? 1:00   yawwwnnn, guess I better get up and freshen my ass up a lil' taste.

He slowly, reluctantly lowered his feet onto the pile carpet, sat on the side of the bed finishing off the dope and looked around his bedroom. Nice,   nice, he thought, checking out the plushness of the deep red, charcoal black and velvet green of the interior.

65

Yeahhhh, really nice   a helluva long way from 42nd and Bowen Avenue, that's for damned sho'!

He burned his right thumb and forefinger slightly on the roach, dropped it in the ashtray and stood up to stretch his lean, even planed six-foot frame, loaded again.

Shit, shower 'n shave. He strolled out of the bedroom heading for his modern gadgeted kitchen, pausing in the living room to open the drapes, to check out what the day was like. Brisk, wind sweeping in from the lake right around the corner, the Northside, only ten niggers in the whole block and three of them hooked up with white broads.

Chili stood straddle-legged, both hands on his slender hips, looking down at the dull, blue-gray streets   uhhh huhhh ... he looked up from under his lids slyly, pinning the two women's faces leering at him from the apartment across the street. Uhhh huhhh, that's right, he nodded to them, what you see is what you get.

They stared boldly at each other for a minute and then pretended that each one's attention was drawn to something else.

Chili slid away from the slit in the drapes, tired of the game, remembering that he wanted a snack.

Bitches! Jive bitches! he muttered, jerking the refrigerator door open.

How long had it been going on? he reflected, the standing-in-the-window-for-the-airline-stewardesses-naked-thing.

Just after I got in here, he answered his thought, pulling out a box of chocolate chip cookies and a wedge of gruyere   six, no, eight months of me exposing my dick to them crazy bitches,   guess I'll hold off for another month and then gon' on over there and fuck everybody in the house, one by one.

The thought caused him to have a semi-erection.

Cynthia! damn!

He snatched a couple cookies from the box and dropped

66

the rest on the kitchen table, rushing to shower and shave, to be smelling good when his main lady, his banker, showed. A leisurely, warm, needle prick shower, a smooth, close shave, a dash of Canoe and the short trip back to the sack for another joint,   a full length tuskie this time.

He carefully arranged himself on top of the covers in his midnight blue, three-quarter length robe, head getting lighter with each hit.

Damnit!   he jerked himself into a sitting position, hopped off the bed mumbling, puffing furiously on the half-smoked joint as he hurried into the living room to put some music on. Leaning over his record racks, he tried to figure out what his mood for music was   something swift by Hubert Laws? Some funky 'Trane? Miles' New Directions? A lil' of the Latin scene with Armando and Mongo? What?

The cold hands over his eyes frightened him so badly for a second that he almost screamed. He recovered quickly, stood up slowly to get his nerves together and turned to face Cynthia Moore, the current sponsor of his lifestyle.

"Cynthia," he gritted his teeth and tried to look down in her face as meanly as possible, "I'm gon' kick your ass one o' these days, doin' that kinda shit to me."

"Scare you?" she asked gaily, pecking him on the chin and tossing her full-length baby calfskin across a nearby chair.

He looked at her tripping around the room, lighting a cigarette, tossing her ash blond, shoulder-length locks over her shoulder, Clairol style.

"Nawww, you didn't scare me, you damned near froze me to death with your cold ass hands," he answered finally, turning away from the sparkling blue eyes, the fading Florida tan, the Norwegian turtleneck and the tailored slacks, to put some music on. He thumbed through the records, feeling, as usual, vaguely irritated that she had a key, a right she insisted on, under the circumstances.

67

"Got any more of that good odor I smell?" she asked over his shoulder as he stuck Black Byrd on the turntable.

"Yeah, look under the bed," he said, placing his roach on the album cover. He watched her twist away to the bedroom as he went in the opposite way to the kitchen. Bitch must be richer 'n Carnation cream. He sliced a couple pieces of cheese and gobbled a couple cookies, stoking up to rap.

"You don't have any rolled?" she called out to him from the bedroom.

"Bring it here!" he called back to her, making his voice sound harsher than he felt.

She turned the corner of the kitchen holding the shoe box, half full of finely grated, stem-free, Laotian marijuana out to him sheepishly.

"You know I just never seem to be able to roll a good joint."

"No, well, where I come from, if you couldn't roll, you couldn't smoke sit down and watch again."

Cynthia Moore, her Gloria Steinem glasses tilted provocatively on her aquiline nose, sat across from him at the kitchen table, her hands folded in her lap like a schoolgirl.

Chili rolled a couple cigarette-sized joints, carefully, pausing at each point in the process to give her the benefit of his expertise. "Now, you do it," he said to her, pushing the box over to her as he lit one.

He sucked in deeply and blew a soft stream of smoke into her face as she fumbled through the process. Bitch buys the best smoke in the world and don't even know how to roll.

Cynthia laughed self-consciously as her sloppily rolled effort fell apart. "Ohhh damnit! I just can't get the hang of it! I guess you have better fingers for this stuff than I do."

"Don't let it ruin your day," he spoke softly to her and handed her his smoke. "No reason why you should be able to do everything good." He watched her puff, knowing she'd be out there in three tokes. "Whatchu been doin' with your-

68

self all week?" he asked, slouching down to let his robe fall open slightly.

She coughed a little of the smoke out, getting up to full lotus her legs under her on the chair.

"Well, Monday I had classes, as you know, . . . yesterday Mother practically forced me to spend the day with her, visiting some perfectly dreadful friends of ours   they have a son," she paused cleverly, took another hit and passed it back to him, "that, well, they've been trying to make the marriage of the season out of for the last three years."

"This the dude with the three names?"

"Yes," she answered, and giggled at the thought . . . Mrs. Stanley Smyth-Frazier.

Chili smiled cynically, watching her blue eyes glaze. "Why don't you wanna get married to the dude, make the ahhemm   marriage of the season?"

Cynthia frowned and accepted the joint, "Don't talk silly, Arnold, please!"

"I'm sorry, baby," he apologized lightly and leaned over to pat her thighs affectionately.

"And you, what've you been doing?"

Chili's mind flashed on the Italian girl's breasts that he had squeezed, mashed and sucked on Monday afternoon, knowing, praying that Cynthia wouldn't come over, and she hadn't   shot to last night's session with the Jewish hippie-artist bitch from the next block.

"Well," he started into his lie carefully, "I told you, at the restaurant Sunday, that I was gon' check out that airlines reservation thing   and I did, but all they seemed to be interested in is whether or not you served honorably in Vietnam." He took the last short length of the joint from her fingers, sliding past everything else, knowing she wouldn't probe too far, even if she was high, because that would make him angry, or sullen, or unaffectionate, or all three.

69

For a year they had been playing this game, and both of them were so good at it by this time, so into where each of them was coming from, that there were seldom any slip-ups.

Cynthia smiled lazily at him. They had an understanding. Black dudes were so groovy, especially dudes like Arnold

"Chili," . . . so full of fire and, at the same time, so helpless, it was like, like you really had to take care of them or they'd be completely lost.

And that's what she did; took care of him, financed his schemes, paid for the sporadic quarters he felt an urge to attend at the various universities around town, his rent, the clothes, his car . . . a noble experiment with a beautiful black animal. What would come out of it, eventually?

Chili uncoiled himself from the chair and stood in front of her, the front of his shortie robe jutting out at her aggressively. How much better could it be? she asked herself, flushing slightly at the uninhibited sight of his erection.

How much better could it be? she reached for his slender brown fingers, a submissive look in her eyes.

Strolling toward the bedroom, arms swathed around each other's waists, she flashed back to the roots of their relationship. Recently resigned from the city's welfare police corps, meaning social work in the ghetto, at an interracial party with a girlfriend, head spaced from two exciting, eerie, weird, frightening, enlightening, erotic years working on the Southside, wondering whether or not it was going to be Europe or Brazil, resisting Mother's insistent pleas that she become a member of the Junior League . . . "Now, Cynthia, . . . you must seriously consider it, for your future social position."

She had stood off to one side, her head bristling with thoughts, twenty-three years old, blond, well-to-do, . . . no, damnit! rich! and be damned, Dad always said

"C'mon, baby . . . dance with me," he had told her, rather than asked, and from there, for the last year, life had been

70

Chili, confusion, fifty-minute sessions. "Don't you see, Miss Moore? don't you understand this need for self-injury?" sex, drugs "Cocaine, girl, cocaine," excitement, games run, a rich fusion of feelings she had felt she was getting as a social worker, but didn't amount to half of what Chili was giving her.

And he was giving her a lot, she felt.

"That ol' smoke done got you fucked up, huh?" he smiled down at her, pulling her sweater up over her head.

She smiled back, unable to speak, her thoughts sweeping her off to obscene feelings about his blackness, the fear and love she felt for him . . . like having your own personal ghetto, she thought, and giggled.

"Yeahhh, you *really* fucked up," Chili said, tossing her sweater into a corner, unpeeling his robe, giving her a show.

Bitch sho' has got a beautiful body.

Chili crawled up into the center of the bed, his eyes pinched into slits from the effect of the herb and watched her unsnap her bra, wade out of her pants and panties.

Bitch sho' has got a beautiful body. I might dig her even if she didn't have no money.

He forced her to stand at the foot of the bed for a minute with a glance, the look appraising her tilted pink nipples, the lush indentation of the waist, the flared, milky thighs and the blond bush filling out the space between her legs like a golden triangle. "C'mere, white woman!" he called to her in a hard, low voice.

Cynthia crawled up into bed beside him, shivering with anticipation. The dug their hands into each other's hair with the first deep kiss, Cynthia moaning, lost already.

Chili opened his eyes as they kissed, studied that lost expression and felt powerful.

"Oohh, Chili   Chili, God! you're so good to me!"

He looked up at the tip of her chin out of the corner of his eye, his mouth gorged with her pink nipple. You mother-

71

fuckin' right I'm good to you, he thought, freaking her out with his lick in the navel technique.

He situated himself in the position that would allow her feverish hands to grasp his joint.

"Heyyyy, be gentle, the baby is awful tender," he whispered up to her as he buried his full lips in her alabaster pussy. The clincher, he thought, swimming his head around between her thighs.

"Oohhh, daddy! daddy! Ooooohhh, daddy! daddy daddy!"

He had touched the money.

A half-hour later, they nodded in each other's arms, Cynthia surreptitiously breathing in Chili's armpit funk, he playing with the long, wispy golden strands of her hair. In the darkened bedroom, far away from his Southside and her Otherside, they traded racial fantasies, turned on by white skin, black skin, pink nipples, black dick, straight hair, nappy hair, expensive perfume, undisguised black funk, different grooves.

"Cynthia, you sleep?"

"No," she answered in a little girl's voice.

"Dig, . . . I don't know if I told you or not, but I been havin' a lil' trouble with my ride, I may need a lil' repair work."

"How much will it cost?"

"Oohhh, three, four-hundred."

Cynthia sighed, recognizing the lie   after all, the car had just had major work done less than a month ago.

"Cynthia!?" he squirmed against her. "Did you hear me, baby?"

"Yesss," she answered quickly, "I heard you. I won't have anything 'til Friday   fathers can be awfully chickenshit sometimes."

He cuddled her closer, sympathetically, relating to her difficulties in life.

72

Yeahhh, you'd have to be sympathetic to a bitch who got a grand a month for an allowance. Plenty sympathetic . . . .

Taco McNeal beamed as she rushed into the house, her arms full of packages.

"Hey, Taco! What is it, baby!" Leo Terry called out to her from the dining room card table.

Slick Rina Dorsey, Taco's roommate, hurried over to help her with the groceries, leaving Leo, Jake the Fake and Harry Mathews at the table.

"Will you look at what the wind blew in here?"

"I see 'em, where you niggers been hidin'?"

"Ain't nobody been hidin'," Jake the Fake answered smoothly, turning his hand down on the table. "I been incarcerated myself."

The group shared a laugh, warm memories linking them up.

Harry winked at Leo before asking, "How in the hell did you manage to walk out with two bags of stuff?"

Taco puffed her full bosom out and announced grandly, "By payin' my hard-earned bread, that's how."

The three men exchanged bewildered expressions.

Jake, playing gun for the other two, "You mean to say you didn't swipe none o' that shit?"

Taco pulled a quart-sized bottle of red wine out of one of the brown bags. "Nope, didn't steal not one cookie, . . . well, I did get one thing for nothin'." She pulled a package of six thinly sliced, loin chops out of her bra.

The group burst into cheers, glad to see that she hadn't completely reformed.

"Yeah! that's my baby!"

"Right on, sister!"

Slick Rina, laughing with the house, passed glasses around for the wine. Harry touched her behind casually with his open palm as she passed him. Slick smiled warmly at him,

73

it had been close to a year now.

Jake the Fake held up his glass for a toast. "Here's to Taco and Slick, two of the downes' sistahs that ever did it, two of the hippes' ladies that it has ever been my purpose to meet and greet, two of . . . ."

"Awww c'mon, Jake, let's play cards . . . She ain't gon' give you none," Leo Terry signified with him, hip to his long-standing crush on Taco.

Jake lowered his glass, pissed at being exposed so ungraciously.

"Yeah, let's play some cards," Taco seconded the motion.

She settled into the seat next to Harry, snatched the deck, collected the cards everyone held, shuffled them and began to deal a whisk hand, as Rina prepared to kibitz.

"What's happenin' to Chili these days?" Jake the Fake asked the general company, trying to bring himself up-to-date on members of their loosely knit fraternity.

Leo glared at the hand Taco had dealt him and winked across to his partner, Harry,   to let him know it was all on him.

"Chili? shit! Chili got some lil' ol' insane white chick out north stuffin' his pockets, buyin' 'im lil' ol' funny cars, sendin' 'im to school 'n I don't know what all."

"Think I'm gon' have to pay that brother a visit," Jake slapped a card down, following suit.

"If you can find 'im," Harry trumped the suit and winked maliciously at his partner.

"Oh, you see him in the neighborhood every now 'n then, flashin', . . . he don't want nobody to know where he's stayin'," Taco added.

They played serious cards for a few hands, slipping up and down the scales of what they had been into over the preceding months.

Jake the Fake, the most recently released from a short stay

74

in the county jail, took advantage of a lull in the game to make a proposal. "Now, dig . . . I know we all been goin' through a bunch o' changes since that bust over on Bowen, but that was a long time ago. I got a surefire scheme that a dude laid on me just before I got out   dynamite! and all it needs is fine players."

Slick Rina winked conspiratorially to Taco and asked, "How would we split the take, Jake?"

"Even steven, baby   even steven."

Leo startled them by popping up from the table as though he'd been pricked. "Hey! what time is it?!"

Jake glared at the interruption. "Damn, man! don't be doin' shit like that!"

"It's seven," Leo announced.

"Father Love is on television tonight."

"Really?"

"You got to be jivin'!"

"No bullshit! They call 'im the Honorable Reverend Father Love these days."

"Yeah, that's right, I read somethin' last week about that jiveass motherfucker."

Taco hurried to the television set in their sparsely furnished front room. "What channel is he on?"

"Two, I think, check the guide," Leo advised her as the small group slid away from the table with their glasses, the card game forgotten, intent on seeing a master player at work.

"What about my thang?" Jake pulled at the group, following them to the front room.

"We can get back to it, Jake   be cool," Taco spoke soothingly to him.

They settled themselves comfortably around the room, watching the t.v. flicker into life.

"Rina, y'all got any smokes?" Harry asked as Father Love strode to the podium behind the opening credits.

Rina reached down under the side of the sofa and pulled out a shoe box lid of seeded, stem scattered weed, her eyes glued to the picture.

"Wait! Lemme make sure the door is locked," Jake said, forcing them all to remember another time, long ago.

"Right on!" Harry encouraged him with a dry smile as they gave the Honorable Reverend Father Love, their undivided attention.

The Honorable Reverend Father Love, a self-styled divinity with an ear for hip sounding titles, stood, holding onto the edges of the podium, very much aware that he was playing super-con for Slick Rina Dorsey, Taco McNeal, Jake the Fake, Harry Mathews, Leo Terry and their ilk. He nodded his fashionably coiffeured noggin in time to the choir's closing notes, a dreamy spiritual number he had written, called "Father's Love."

"Lookit that motherfucker style!" Jake the Fake called out with pure admiration, a critic of the highest order.

"Yeah, ain't he somethin'?" Slick Rina responded from across the room.

Everyone in the room leaned forward a bit as Father Love opened his mouth to spiel.

"Sisters   sisters 'n brothers," he began, surveying his docile, responsive audience, grabbing hold of the flight of nerves that the cocaine he had snorted just before showtime took him on. "Sisters 'n brothers   the Lawwwd works in mysterious ways," he announced grandly, jutting his chin out with Mussolinian cockiness. The chorus of amens! and right ons! that greeted his announcement caused Leo Terry to spill his wine, laughing.

"Hahhh hah hahhh ha ha ha ... mannnnn! will you listen to that shit! That motherfucker ain't even changed his rap for t.v.! Wowwww!"

76

"Shhhhhhhhhhhhh!"

"Yes, sisters 'n brothers, the Lawd works in mysterious ways,   there are times when some of us don't even think that He's workin' at all, but I, the Honorable Reverend Father Love, can assure you that He is."

Harry stood and made a little Flip Wilson-Geraldine movement in affirmation, "What you see is *not* what you get wowwweeee!"

"Sit yo' ass down, Harry 'n behave," Taco cautioned him, "watchin' one fool at a time is enough."

Rina continued rolling the dope and passing it out.

"There are many reasons why I can assure you of the Lawd's workin's, but," and here Father Love turned his well-shaped mustache toward camera number two, a close shot, "I shall only use one example, due to the lack of time we have here on television."

He paused theatrically, to let it fully seep into the minds of his followers that he and, by extension, they were on television.

"Uhhh huhhh, nice, Father, nice," Jake mumbled.

"Five years ago, or a little less, I was uhhh . . . what some folks would call   down 'n out. I say, hah hah   some folks would call it down 'n out, I never would. At that time, I was lackin' many of the necessities one needs to do the work of the Lawd. I must confess to you here in the audience, sisters 'n brothers, and to those of you out there in video land, that I was becomin' depressed, blue, saddened by the adversities that life was layin' on me."

"Play, Daddy Love! play!"

"But!" he stabbed a glittering, diamond decked forefinger, "I knew I had the Lawd's work to do, so therefore nothin' I say, nothin'! was goin' to keep me feelin' low for very long. We'll pause right here for a couple commercial messages, and then I'll tell y'all what pulled me through."

77

Taco moved quickly to turn the sound of the commercials off and looked around at the group, bubbling with sarcasm and admiration.

"You believe that!?" Slick Rina looked around her with a dry curl to her mouth.

"Motherfuckin' right, I believe it," Leo responded. "He's gettin' over, ain't he?"

"What's his money pitch?" Jake asked, a professional's interest drowning out emotional considerations.

"Let's listen 'n see."

Taco turned the sound back up and slumped down in front of the set, toking up meditatively.

"Now then, as I was sayin', just before the commercial break, money may or may not be the root of all evil, but it certainly can be the cause of a lot of hardship if you don't have any."

Jake and Harry, verbal switcheroo artists from wayyy back, exchanged looks and silently slapped each other's palms in recognition of where the Father had taken things to.

"When I didn't have the church I have now, the physical manifestation of God's presence, when I didn't have the nursin' home for the aged, that uhhh . . . we have now, when I didn't have the money to pay for prime time to get the message out to the greatest number of people, I was sad. That, sisters 'n brothers, and y'all out there in video land, is what made me sad . . . not my own personal problems, no sir, no m'am, they never counted, my concern has always been, how am I goin' to find the way to spread the Lawd's Word? Prices being what they are today.

"A lot of people don't think we're supposed to talk about earthly things in religion, in sermons, . . . they'd like to keep everything in the clouds. Well, all I can say to them is this, what ye reap, so shall ye sow, and vice versa. If you want a lot, you have to give a lot, that's both heavenly and earthly."

78

"Dig 'im! dig 'im!" Jake pointed excitedly at Father Love's eye-rolling to the sky.

"We see 'im, Jake, shit! be cool!"

"The main purpose of my program," Father Love continued, having unsettled most of his audience with his deliberately contrived detour, a trick used to make them wander a bit and accept his exit sign ... this way, please   "is to help all of us who can believe in the Lawd and my work,

by that I mean this, it means givin' up those petty concerns for personal problems, we have the answers for those problems. Yes, sisters 'n brothers, we do. Don't worry about those anymore.

"The concern that we should have is not for those petty things but for other things, such as ... how can I make this a better world? Or if I can't do it, or I don't know how to begin, how can I help that individual who does know?"

Father Love disguised his frown of irritation at the sound of the choir backing him up a paragraph too soon. They had been told not to drown his request for donations out with a bunch of tambourines shaking.

"You, you, and especially you, can help make this a better world," he intoned solemnly, pointing his finger at the television audience. "Send whatever you can afford to: The Honorable Reverend Father Love's Better World Foundation, Box 369, Chicago, Illinois, zip code 60011. I will leave you now, to return to your homes and your hearts this same time next week, the Lawd willing. To those of you who tuned in late, I would like to repeat, donations should be sent to the Honorable Reverend Father Love's Better World Foundation, Box 369, Chicago, Illinois   zip 60011."

He placed his palms together, the slender, bejeweled fingers pointing heavenward, and repeated, "That address, once again, is the Honorable Reverend Father Love's Better World Foundation, Box 369, Chicago, Illinois   zip code 60011

We are a non-sectarian organization, dedicated to the ideal of peace on earth and good will toward all men, black and white. I thank you for havin' allowed me to come into your homes and hopefully your hearts this evenin', to bring you my understandin' of the Lawd's Words. I leave you with this last message   This *can* be a better world, with love."

Slick Rina, Taco, Harry, Leo and Jake the Fake stared at the television as though they were hypnotized.

Leo whistled as an announcer, voice over the credits, requested again, "Donations should be sent to the Honorable Reverend Father Love's Better World Foundation, Box 369, Chicago, Illinois   zip code 60011   that's the Honorable Reverend Father Love's Better World Foundation, Box 369, Chicago, Illinois, zip code 60011   Thank you and remember   this *can* be a better world, with love."

Slick Rina shook her head from side to side, making a profound gesture of disbelief. "You mean to tell me that this . . . this . . . this monkey time, pootbutt, jiveass motherfucker is gettin' away with that?"

"Clean as a whistle."

"Well, I'll be goddamned."

"Ain't but one thing wrong with his thang," Jake shot in professorially.

"What's that, professor Fake?" Harry punned on his nickname.

"His organization's name is too long."

"Yeahhh, you got a point there," Harry conceded, backing off from the fun thing.

"He's gettin' away   with that?" Rina spoke out again, in something akin to absolute wonder.

"Honey," Taco purred to her roommate, "if you don't know how gullible people can be, nobody knows."

"I can dig where you comin' from   but goddamn! you mean to tell me that all you have to do is rent some television

80

time, make up a meaningless, bullshit talk and then ask people to send you money? Is that all?"

"I know an easier way to do it, and you don't even have to get on t.v.," Jake slid in smoothly, certain of everyone's attention now.

The other people in the room, the larceny in their blood stirred up by Father Love's charlatanism on the tube, looked at him expectantly.

Chapter 4
Forks in the Road

Chester L. Simmons, alias the Great Lawd Buddha, stood off by himself in a corner of the exercise yard, warming his cold bones in the bright autumn sun and reading a letter, over and over, from Billy Woods, an ex-member of the Afro-Lords. He smiled at Billy's description of his first child, "a rubber facced, brown bouncer of a baby boy."

The Great Lawd Buddha finished the letter finally and tilted his face up toward the sun, slanted eyes closed, soaking in the warmth. Life in the joint wasn't so bad, he rationalized for a moment, the sun's rays tripping him out, not if you had three squares a day, few hassles and a chance to write as much as you wanted.

He slowly lowered his head, his prison issued baseball cap shrouding his face with shadows. No, he scratched his earlier thought, no, that's not right . . . being in jail is pure idee hell. He looked out across the yard, his eyes sweeping across a panorama of misery, self hate, inhumane cruelty, dumb rage, social fiction and human degradation.

Chester L. Simmons, the Great Lawd Buddha, Mississippian, Black brotherman, poet, dramatist, world spieler, artist, speculator, murderer.

His thoughts twisted away from the snake pit scene in front of him, back in time, to his life with Josie "Heatwave" Masterson, the one-time apple of his eye, the lady who made him blow his cool   six times into her body with a German luger.

Why did it have to be Josie? Why Josie? he'd asked himself a dozen profound times, behind a terrible day under a sadistic bull, or after a dismal night dreaming of the flavor of her body's juices, the warmth of her eyes, her nose, her lips, her neck, her beautiful titties, her stomach, her hips, the lovely grizzled pussy between her thighs, her magnificent ass   thoughts that took him beyond momentary unpleasantries, like doing twenty to life.

But, life being what it is, he philosophized, it had to be Josie   c'est la vie.

He plunged his hands deeper into his pockets, the anguish of five-thousand hours of remorse tilting his face back up into the sun, seeking warmth, oblivion from haunted memories.

They were on him before he was aware of their presence.

"Whass happenin', bruh Buddha?" the boldest of the trio entree'd.

He pinned all three lazily. Tough, hip, literate, now-type young niggers, into books 'n politics. Good.

"Nothin' to it, lil' brothers, a baby could do it."

He leaned against the cement wall at his back and crossed his legs. Which one would it be?

"Buddha, what's this shit I hear 'bout you being a white

84

man in South Africa?" Marcus, the bank robber, asked point blank, and knelt to hear the full story.

"Ohhh, that," Buddha super-casually tossed off and folded himself down slowly into his sumo wrestling rest stance, glad to talk a lil' shit to open minds.

"That . . . hah hah . . . that was the result of a most weird set of circumstances, most weird. If I could possibly bum a cigarette from one of you three golden brothers, I would be most happy to run the whole thing down to you."

Marcus held the pack of Benson and Hedges out to him immediately, pleased to be able to supply his need. One could never tell, one day it might be candy, one day nutmeg, snuff or cocaine, but most often, Benson and Hedges.

"It all started after I had to make my European break, behind my heroin thang; I told you all about that, didn't I? being hounded by those Algerian mafia dudes over that kilo?"

The three men nodded solemnly, one of their favorites.

"O.k., there I was, once again, on a freighter   I used to go a lotta places on freighters, this time as a common seaman. I had stolen a Malay seaman's documents, on my way to wherever the brute that I was treadin' water on was headed. Now why we had to wind up in Capetown, South Africa, is something that only God above and the captain of the sleazy bitch we was sailin' on could answer.

"Cape-town, South Af-ri-ca," he enunciated syllable by syllable, as though grinding his teeth on something bitter.

"I'll never know why, what it was that caused me to jump ship in a place like that, but there I was, on my ass in Capetown. In many ways I can say to you, unequivocally, that it was one of the grooviest black places I've ever been in this world. I mean, like sho' 'nuff groovy gut bucket black. Everybody underneath white, that is to say, the Coloreds, Cape Malays, Indians, Zulus, Xosas, Basuto, everybody else after white helped everybody else. I had some dudes help put to-

85

gether all the documents I needed, just to walk the streets. I had people feed me, pass me around like I was a cookie that might crumble up in their hands." His voice rumbled dramatically. "I was a soul brother from the U-nited States who had decided to stay with them in their locations, share their oppression. Beautiful people, gentlemen, beautiful people, carved out of love." He accepted the pre-offered cigarette and carried on, caught up by his story.

"I had three families slip me around in their location for two months, just ahead of the state police, the Gestapo is really what they were.

"Now dig it! I feel I must elaborate on this point because it is most important. I was a potentially dangerous, slick-minded U-nited States nigger who had jumped ship for subversive reasons, and was known to do my share of dirt, that is, if the truth be known."

Donnell, Marcus and Brian all held their hands out to be slapped, their common sense of wrongdoing embroidered for them in a way that they had never heard it before.

"The South African police, brothers," he continued more slowly, deeply, "the South African police could bring pee to a chump's eyes, if they caught you gettin' down wrong, missin' a step or doin' any other such shit as they could misconstrue being against their regime. And there I was, young, foolish, wild, so crazy that I didn't even know why I had jumped ship.

"Some of the militant brothers thought I had come over secretly as a black Che Guevara, but actually, if y'all want to hear the truth, what happened was this: I had gotten off into a thang with a bitch who was part Kalahari Bushwoman and part Cape Malay, and she was so fine that I decided to stay with her, no matter what. Nobody had told me too much about the racial setup, nobody had told me that the Afrikaners discriminated against everybody, even they own mommas."

86

The trio laughed indulgently, pulling their collars up against the deepening chill.

"Yeahhh, thass right! Even they own mommas! There was a case, while I was there, of a police inspector who caught his momma with the yard 'boy' and was so outraged that he had the Racial Classification Board declare his mother one piece nigger, shifted her away from him, had the Re-classification Board bypass him as a nigger and kept on livin' happily ever after with his snow white wife. Helluva country! I'm tellin' ya! Helluva country!"

Marcus nodded in serious agreement, his reading having covered the South African sickness, its cancer.

"After a bit, some of the dudes who were lookin' out for me, at the risk of their lives, helped get me a gig   down in the diamond mines."

"Diamond mines?!" Donnel showed the gold caps on his teeth in surprise.

"That's what you heard, amigo   diamonds! diamonds!" the Great Lawd Buddha licked his lips and sparkled his eyes in the oblique rays of the sun, caricaturing greed. "Every morning at 4:30 a.m., we slaves, yeahhh, that's just about what we were, slaves   makin' so little a day, when you think about how much income we were makin' for the Baas, translated meanin' Boss. But actually goin' deeper than that 'cause they had a system based on that Baas thing called Baaskap or Baaskamf or something like that, that was supposed to keep black people 'n everybody else un-white underground for the rest of their lives, and after they died, they'd bury 'em there."

Marcus jammed his hands deeper into his blue denim jacket pocket and scowled at the wall above Buddha's head. "Sounds like Mississippi or New York, don't it?"

"Really!" Donnell affirmed, quietly slapping Buddha's outstretched palm.

"But actually it was worse than that. Much worse. At any rate, I'm down underneath the ground, siftin' diamonds up big as your fist, turnin' each 'n everyone into the Baas, 'til one day my dirty, treacherous, U-nited States nigger mind started shootin' off sparks. I knew, from havin' watched it, that some of the dudes managed to get away with a tiny bit o' stuff every month, industrial type diamonds, mostly. What I wanted to do was cop some authentic gems, some real stones.

"So, I got to work. It was really hard for awhile, to get my organization together. I mean, like a few of the more un-sophisticated African brothers didn't even feel that it was right to steal from the Baas."

"Buddha! you gotta be jivin'!"

"I wouldn't jive you, youngblood," he answered his critic with a deadpan under his cap.

"But you see, their minds were formed in a tribal mold, they didn't think it was right to steal from *any-body*, and to lots of them, despite the fact that they suffered under him, the white man was still a human being.

Deep, huh? probably one of the main reasons why all those black folks over there haven't lynched all those white folks. At any rate, after a lil' bit, I escaped from the mines . . ."

"Escaped?" Brian asked.

"Uhhhh huhhhnnn, E-scaped. You see, at that time, you signed a contract for two years, one year or whatever, and the only way you could break your contract was to E-scape. I escaped and became a fence for the dudes I had organized in the mines.

"My thang went a lil' bit like this, I'd pay about fifty dol-lars for a helluva gem, one-hundred, U.S. rates, for a fantas-tic gem and two-hundred, at least, for one of those over-whelming pinkie rings that you sometimes see on the small

88

fingers of eminent sissies and stark ravin' rich Harlem pimps."

His audience held onto each other, their attention to his tale forcing them to disregard customary no-nos.

"I moved fast, bought everything that I could get my hands on, dealt with a rich ol' Jewish diamond merchant who had an interest in the mines that the stones were being ripped off from. Now he really had a thang goin' on. He couldn't lose for winnin'   makin' dough out of both ends.

"You dudes ever see a diamond merchant?"

The three men mechanically nodded no in unison.

"Well, take my word for it, they, 'long with the diamond cutters, are weird lookin' lil' bitty dudes. They all got pointed heads, they're usually bald and they don't have no emotion whatsoever and would do anything   I mean, anything for diamonds. The dude I was dealin' with, tryin' to pull a super-grand stake together, in order to split the scene, tried to have me arrested a couple times, and when that didn't work, tried to have me assassinated. All he cared about was the diamonds   yeah, that's all."

He stood up to stretch his legs and eased back down into position, his belly hanging over his belt, Sumo style. "Anyway, within six months I had scrounged up 'bout $600,000 worth o' diamonds, some really good 'n some really bad, and I was gettin' ready to hat up   but, as Lady Luck would have it, the night before I got ready to split, I was leavin' a Xosa lady's crib, a too-fine fine lady named Christa, at 12:30 a.m., and got picked up for a pass violation   and that's when the shit hit the fan."

Buddha paused to nod solemnly to six members of a Chicano group to whom he had given a Third World talk to, the day before. "Yeahhh, the shit sho' 'nuff hit the fan," he continued. "Number one, the police must've spent three or four months grillin' me, tryin' to make me tell them who the white man was behind my organization. The more I told them that

89

I was, the less they believed me.

"Finally, it dawned on one of those superduper crackers that I was actually the Head Nigger in Charge. Now that really twisted their lil' ol' hate-filled minds around. Me, Chester L. Simmons from Miss'ssippi, one of their sister states, had actually been behind some grand theft action   it was too much for 'em!

"Now what they did, some bureaucrat in the Racial Determination section, was this. Since it was obvious that no black man could possibly have schemed himself into the kind of dough I was into, or created the kind of structured stealin' that I had created,   then I must be a white man."

"Wowwww! Talk about goin' through changes!" Marcus burst out, eyes digging the Great Lawd.

"Hmf! Changes you say? Uhhn huh, as good a word for it as you could hope to use. What was happenin', aside from all the money I was usin' to bribe everybody and his brother with, was this. On the socio-political propaganda side, the authorities didn't want any kind of word to leak out officially about my gettin' past the diamond mine check system. Me, a black dude! I mean, like, after all, that would give a lot o' people big ideas. So, therefore, in that typical iron-headed way they have of doin' things in that fucked up country, they had me declared a white man. Can you git ready for that?"

"You a bad dude, Buddha," Donnell assured him.

"By this time I'd been in the slams, in solitary for about six months, but my money was workin' for me. I managed to stick coin to the Prime Minister's uncle even . . . anything to get out. Now, young brothers, I'll tell you the truth, if I'm lyin' I hope God'll strike me dead."

He paused for a cigarette and a light, dragged in.

"I don't know who really decided that the best thing to do was deport me, but I sho' wanna thank him. Aside from my bribery, they wanted to get rid of me for political reasons.

90

They didn't want a declared white man that looked kind o' black in jail creating some weird kind of martyr for the black people, so they forced me to agree to a deportation scene.

"Well, heyyy, you can imagine how I felt. I would've agreed to anything to get out of that place. Anything!"

"Right on, brother!" Brian cued in.

"Well, you can believe they fucked me over a lil' bit before I was finally released. One day the guard would announce that I was leavin' that evenin', then turn right back around and tell me to forget about it . . . as well as your other kinds of regular torture. The South African white man is a stranger to most of the rest of the human race, him and the rednecked Mississippian. I don't really know what happened to them durin' the evolutionary process, but I do know this, a special kind of sickness settled into them hundreds of years ago and they've never been close to being healthy."

The Great Lawd Buddha pursed his lips reflectively and slowly stood, his eyes following the lazy flight of a pigeon. Marcus, Donnell and Brian followed the direction of his eyes.

Brian, impatiently wanting to hear the end of Buddha's story before lockup, asked "Uhh, so they booted you out, huh?"

"In the dead of night, my friend, in the dead of night," he continued, snapping his eyes away from the pigeon's flight, "me and three other undesirable aliens. However, I could say, as a history maker, that I had had the opportunity to be a black white man in one of the most prejudiced white places on earth, and you can believe me, that takes some doin'.

"Awright, deported, hardshippin' and in Zambia, tryin' to shit out a few of these gems I'd stuffed away in my precious lil' body."

"You got away with some?"

"Clean as a whistle! They'd made me take some laxatives 'n shit, but years ago, in India, that's another whole story, a great Yoga man taught me how to control my bowels. I

91

mean, like I once knew how to half-shit or fart at three different tonal levels, and a whole bunch of other things, but you know how it is if you don't practice.

"At any rate, I was home free, a pocket full of precious stones, off to trade with the Conquerin' Lion of Judah, the King of Kings, His Imperial Lawdship, Haile Selassie himself."

"Oh wowwww!"

"Yessuh! I figured that the only righteous dude I could deal with would be the Emperor of Ethiopia. I knew, if anybody had any dough at all, it would be him   so off I go to Ethiopia."

The guard on the tower station above them, concerned about lengthening shadows and the intensity of their closeness, motioned them out to the center of the yard.

Marcus scowled up at the guard. "Hey, I got a lil' home brew in my cell, y'all wanna ...?"

"No sooner said than done!" Buddha agreed quickly, the last rays of the sun disappearing over the wall, chilling him to the bone.

The four of them made their way through the relays of contraband searchers, up to their tier.

Marcus ushered them into his cell as though he were receiving guests in a swank house. "Make yourselves to home. It ain't much but it all belongs to the state."

He uncovered a potent half-pint of distilled potato drippings, rubbing alcohol, iodine (for color) and the residue of several past batches and passed it to the guest of honor.

"Ooooowhhheeeeeee!" Buddha exclaimed, squinching up his already squinched up eyes. "Godddammmm! This shit is *ugly*!" He passed his critique on it and took another long swallow. The trio beamed around him.

"Go on, Buddha, you was in Ethiopia."

"Uh huh, sho' was. Got a fair and square deal on my gems

92

from His Majesty, hung around Addis Ababba long enough to sock a couple crumbcrushers into a few ladies and departed, ten minutes ahead of three tribes of brothers intent on makin' me marry their sisters and a red hot case of ol' fashioned plague."

Donnell spilled a little of the home brew down the side of his jaw. "What kinda plague?"

"The bubonic plague, young suh, the bubonic plague. The kind that they used to have in Europe that would kill off half of London or Paris or Amsterdam. The plague plague.

"But like I said, I was off. What I was goin' to do was hit off 'round the eastern coast, shoot through the Upper Suedan right quick, slice through Egypt   I hadn't been to Cairo yet, whip 'round the edge of Libya, maybe get on back into Europe from Algeria, if everything was cool.

"As it turned out, everything was love jones, 'til I got to Algeria. Somebody had put out a contract on my ass. I don't have to tell you who, and I guess it was stupid of me to be thinkin' that the Algerians who wanted my nuts wouldn't check back home every now and then.

"Anyway, whilst I was dodgin' knives, bullets and shit being dropped from rooftops, they had started another one of those lil' ol' funny time wars they were in the habit of startin'. I think this one was about some dude snatchin' some other dude's woman's veil off."

"Pass it on, Donnell!" Brian reminded him, as he stared hypnotically into Buddha's mouth.

Buddha accepted the half empty, half-pint bottle and bowed while seated, supergraciously, half lit.

"I got out," he said curtly, after a quick swallow. "Who has our cigarettes?"

Marcus lit a Benson 'n Hedges and handed it to him respectfully.

"Yeah, I got out, fled to Casablanca, Morocco. Now that's

93

a town for you if ever there was one! At the time I swooped in, everything went! You hear me, lil' brothers! Everything!! I hadn't been in town fifteen hot minutes, black in white, white on black, moppin' my face with a snow white hankerchief, when two of the most beautiful lil' girls, teenagers actually

'bout fourteen 'n fifteen, grabbed me to lead me to their virgin mother."

The men winked across the booze and their male feelings for those games.

"What could I say? What could I do? I 'married' all three of 'em that weekend and settled down to a harmonious domestic life. I must hasten to add, right in through here however, that the kind of domestic life I had wasn't all that domestic. Within three months I had gotten my pinkie finger into the hash trade, had my big toe in the cocaine thing and was handlin' a few choice gems. I had learned a whole lot about how to judge a stone from the ol' pointy headed diamond merchant, and the rest of me was pushed off into them French diplomats' wives,   those that had a lil' somethin' to add to the family treasury.

"But, as usual, I got greedy. The more I had, the more I wanted. I tried to corner the hash market, and the king got salty and kicked me out. He really, actually was usin' my dealin's as an excuse. What he really wanted was my woman, Fatima."

The Great Lawd Buddha uncoiled himself slowly from Marcus' bunk, stood looking through the barred Gothic window, remembering. When he spoke again, after long moments of deep thought, his voice, a sound track of his experiences in life, carried the flavor of the souk, the yearning cry of the kif fiend, the smoke and intrigue of North Africa.

"Fatima   Fatima," he spoke her name reverently, as though whispering into the Prophet's ear. "So beautiful, so deep and so arrogant that when she walked through the streets

94

. . . pin-striped tattoo blued from her chin to her bottom lip, dudes used to walk into the sides of the buildings, or start prayin' right on the spot. And Aissa and Naima were just about as fine as their mother. So much of what was happenin' to me in those days was so mysterious, so unbelievable. Like Fatima and her daughters, for example.

"And I had to leave it all," he said suddenly and remounted his seat of honor. "Yep, once again I had to leave it or run the risk of being drowned by the king's men in a sand dune somewhere."

"Hey Marcus, you got any black shoe polish?" a fellow con leaned into the cell door.

Marcus frowned, nodded no and tried to wave him away, but the brother, peeking in, caught up by the rapt expressions on everyone's face, eased in and squatted at the foot of Marcus' bunk.

Buddha, Algerian flamenco, wavy blue sand, home brew, Rabat, Marrakesh, Casablanca and Fatima sizzling through his imagination, merely nodded at the brother and rapped on. "After my expulsion I became a lost man. It was as though my senses didn't want to work anymore, as though too much had happened. It was terrible, purely and simply terrible, my brothers. I became a soulless, ash-splattered, piss-stained, dodo-covered representative of humanity, sleeping wherever my head found itself, eatin' goat turds and rat shit, searchin' for my Self again."

The latest addition to the group looked from one face to the other, seeking some explanation for where they were, but receiving none, listened harder.

"If you can get into what my trip was. Here I had been declared a white man in South Africa, managed to avoid the perils of being lynched, had made it around the eastern fringe of Momma Africa and all of a sudden, for only reasons that the Great It has an explanation for, I find myself in rags,

95

walkin' down through Mauritania, tryin' my goddamnest to get to someplace on the west coast, to get on a freighter, or a slaveship, or somethin', headed for the Indies, at least. My luck had run out, and I knew it."

He turned the bottle up and sipped delicately, as though it were his by reason of possession   no one bothered to correct him.

"I still had a diamond big enough to constipate an elephant in my rags, but I was savin' that for the finale, for my grand exit from Africa. What I had in mind to do was drop it in the Atlantic, a hardened tear for the souls of all our brothers 'n sisters who had jumped, been pushed, or had in some way, wound up being shark's grub for a few hundred years durin' the black human being trade."

Marcus, an Ourstorian, looked at the Great Lawd Buddha with a tearful gleam in his eye, the home brew almost pushing it out.

"In Africa, amongst the religious people, you always pour what they call a libation to the gods on every occasion. That's what I had planned to do. But, as usual, Mr. Fate spread his fingers all over my plans and took me off.

"I wouldn't even attempt to try to take you dudes through all the supernatural trips, all the days 'n nights of starvation, both physical and spiritual, the times I was lost amongst people who thought I was a god, or a dog, or any of that   all of the moments of intense ecstasy and profound sadness I experienced durin' my two-year walk."

"Two year walk?!" the newcomer exclaimed.

"Shut up, Amos," Brian said quietly, brutally.

"Yeah, two years I walked," Buddha favored him with a wise old glance, "from the outskirts of Casablanca, through what they used to call the Spanish Sahara, Mauritania, Senegal, Guinea, Liberia, the Ivory Coast   on into Ghana.

"Now strangely enough, for some reason, by the time I

96

made it to Ghana, my mind seemed to clear itself, to come alive again. All of a sudden it seemed that I was amongst *my* people. Can y'all get into where I'm comin' from?"

All four men, his audience, nodded yes, yes, yes, yes.

"I don't know what it was, really. Maybe it was that cup of twenty-five year old palm wine a sister on the outskirts of Accra laid on me, or the words of an American blood who spoke to me or whatever, but I was back in the world uhh huhh . . . back in the world. Naturally I wound up dealin' with the slickest motherfuckers in six countries for this stone I had. Got a decent price for it too, went out and bought some hip kente cloth robes, partied a lil' bit and the next thing I know, the Asantehene of the Ashanti people is requesting the pleasure of my appearance.

"The Asantehene! If you don't know who he is, I can't begin to tell you. All I can say is this: when the Asantehene wants you, you wind up being where he wants you. He's sorta like part god and part African.

"So there I am, in a huge room with the Asantehene and his linguist, that's the dude who does all his rappin' for him. The Asantehene is sittin' on a golden throne, with gold strands of thread hangin' down over his face, a couple gold nuggets weighin' his fingers down, gold woven into his robes. Gold, damnit! Everywhere! And the linguist, a hip lil' ol' dude 'bout sixteen years older 'n' Damballah is rappin' to me, tellin' me that the Asantehene wants me to find the Golden Stool for him.

"He wants me, you dig?! Chester L. Simmons, to find the Golden Stool for him. I almost shat granola crumbs when I heard that. Why me? And then the Asantehene spoke, or rather threw his voice from over in a corner, must've been a ventriloquist . . . dude had a voice like a bass conga drum.

" 'I have followed your movement around the outer edges of our continent, I know of your spiritual battles, what you have suffered and overcome,' he says to me in letter-perfect, hightoned English, 'and it is for these reasons that I ask you to find the soul of my nation.'

"Behind that he didn't say another mumbling word, he just sat there, just as cool and serene as you please. The linguist held a medium-sized leather pouch out to me, and I crawled out on my hands and knees, the way I'd crawled in. I mean, like that's the way you came to the Asantehene.

"Once I got outside, about five blocks from the palace, I opened the strings to the pouch and discovered it was filled with gold dust. Gold dust! I was shitless speechless. It was like . . . it was like the Lawd had asked you to find his favorite pillow and paid you out front for it.

"Now the thing was, I couldn't say anything to anybody because nobody was supposed to know that the Stool was missin'.

"I mean, like if the Stool was missin' people would start dyin' off, out of sadness or whatever, 10,000 natural catastrophes would occur, in addition to the fact that the Asantehene would be lynched in fifty different ways, along with every member of his family, and his name would be in the books forever as the dude who blew the Stool. You talk about a motherfucker in serious trouble!

"I ain't talkin' 'bout him, I'm talkin' about me!

"If I succeeded in recoverin' the Stool, no one but the Asantehene and his linguist would know about it. If I didn't recover the Stool, my ass would be in a sling, six feet under, and no one would know about that either.

"I was so shook up that I went off and drank pink gin for two weeks, tryin' to find the vision for what I was supposed to be doin'."

He turned the corner of the bottle up and killed it, so into his story that he had forgotten about the other people in the cell. "Oooopps, sorry 'bout that!" he apologized graciously.

98

"Fuck that, man! Go on, what happened?!" Marcus shot in.

"Well, once I got my head together, I started gettin' the kind of logical vibes I needed. By way of the process of elimination, I figured out certain things. Number one, no Ashanti would be caught dead or alive with the Stool; their uhhh sensibilities just wouldn't know how to deal with it. It would be like havin' God's ghost locked up in the closet. I was pretty certain that none of the other tribal groups had copped the Stool because if they had . . . hah hah hah well, if they had, they would've had a war on their hands that would've been guaranteed annihilation for everybody, forever. And ever.

"O.k., havin' gone up 'n down, and in 'n out in my head, who could I settle down on that would be insensitive enough, disrespectful enough, vicious enough and cold-blooded enough to rip off the soul of a nation?

"The white boy!" Brian called out.

The Great Lawd Buddha leaned over unsteadily, the potato drippings singing in his skull, to slap Brian's palm suavely. "Right on, brother! The white boy! Now I really had a problem. The English, the white boy in charge at that time didn't dig me being in the country in the first place, and if I made any too wrong moves, my ass was gon' be in another sling, so I had to proceed quietly."

The sound of a fellow inmate screaming on the tier below them sliced through Buddha's narrative. They all tensed up. They knew the sound well. Someone receiving a "Dear John" letter, or suddenly being overcome by the pressure of the cage surrounding him or from a thousand other prisoned feelings had gone insane. The man below them, his lungs suddenly lined with steel, screamed 'til the keepers finally arrived, billy clubs and gas guns at the ready, prepared to beat and gas and drag him off to the Hole, for "rehabilitation."

Buddha accepted another cigarette, his hands shaking

99

slightly, aware of the importance of having something complete happen, especially where they were. "As we all know, money talks, all kinds o' money. So that's what I put to work for me. That and my game.

"It took me something like four months to find out how many, which and where foreign archeological expeditions had been, or was diggin'. I had cornered things down to that point. Since no one had ever seen the Stool, other than the Asantehene, I figured that some fool archeologists, rapin' the country like they was doin' in those days, had stumbled across the piece and was definitely keepin' it cool 'til they got it out of the country.

"Usin' the elimination process again, I sifted the expeditions ... a French group, an Italian group, a Portuguese group, of all things, and about eight English groups, naturally.

"Gentlemen, you talkin' 'bout a dude earnin' his dust! I sho' 'nuff earned mine that year. I got to the Stool, all boxed and on its way to Rome, the day before the S.S. Aida sailed.

"What I did was this: I found out that the Italians had stumbled across the Stool, which was buried, had lied to the English colonial master guys about what they had found and was gettin' ready to arrivederci.

"Awright, playin' the game, I managed to slip word in to the Englishman in charge. Naturally he's pissed. I mean, like they were gonna put all the dagos in jail 'n shit, ... but what he was really happy about was gettin' his grubby hands on the Stool.

"As y'all know, the goddamned English had fought a war with the Ashanti over the Stool, years back, so they really felt groovy about gettin' their hands on something that they'd fought like dogs for. But heyyy, this *is* the Great Lawd Buddha, right?!"

"Right on, Buddha! right on!" Brian yelled, oblivious to his surroundings.

100

"Yessuhhh, so what I did, with about eight of the most nervy Ashanti dudes you ever thought about hearin' about, was perform the most perfectly executed robbery in the history of the country. One of the dudes who helped me rip the Stool off later became a cabinet minister, or the chief justice, or something like that, after Ghana got independent. The dudes who helped to pull the job off didn't even want to get paid. I had to make them take some dust.

"My con to them was, you dig? I want you all to help me pull off a fantastic, incredible, unreal, daylight savin's time holdup on the English.

"That's all I had to say to those dudes, that's all   that we were goin' to embarrass the English so bad that they would be walkin' 'round with red faces for days. And that's what we did, I organized   on the q.t., of course, a tribal festival that involved the Asantehene. And while he was layin' his blessings on the buildin' the festival revolved around, with the Duke and the Duchess, the King's representatives in attendance

"This is what we did. At the high point of things, my hip Ashanti buddies eased off with the Stool in a crate, singin' 'n drummin' 'n shit, in the middle of about fifty 'leven million fellow tribesmen.

"I'll never know for certain, but I think   I say I think the English knew what was goin' down but they couldn't scream, 'Hey! bring that bloody Stool back!' 'cause they couldn't admit they had it, not with all those brothers out there. On the other hand, the Asantehene couldn't admit that he was stealin' it back 'cause he was never supposed to have lost it in the first place.

"We wound up with what you might call an impass. Three days later, the Asantehene called me in again, laid another bag o' dust on me without sayin' nary a word; two days after that the English 'advised' me to get on. Or, as I remember

101

the way the young stud put it, 'Uhh, Simmons, we should like to see you depart on the next scheduled ship from this ahrea.'

"When's that? I asked him.

" 'This afternoon,' he told me and didn't blink once.

"So, once again,   there I was, orphaned in the world."

He stood and stretched, "Yeahhhh, orphaned in the world." He bowed to the men in the cell like a Mandarin lord and strolled out onto the tier, heading for his own cell, and the horrors awakened within himself from a couple hours of story telling.

"Buddha!?" Marcus called to him as he made his exit.

He turned, two cells away   a quizzical expression on his Mao-shaped face.

"Buddha, you ever think about doin' your autobiography?"

Buddha smiled at him coldly. "Yeah, I did do it once. It got all messed up, that's why I'm servin' time now."

Marcus looked down at the floor helplessly, and then back up to see Buddha disappear into his own cell, ready for the evening lockup.

Sweet Peter Deeder sat in the corner of the sofa in his eighth floor apartment, a drink beside him, a three-hole notebook on his robed lap, looking out at the twinkling lights of the city.

What was coming up? Another lecture tour, a few t.v. talk-show shots, a best selling underground record album (Sweet Peter Raps), a couple other lil' things, a movie role, possibly.

He took a long sip from his drink. So much had happened to turn his head around. He smiled solemnly at the memory of the brutal ass-kicking Kwendi and company had given him years back. Maybe they did me a favor, maybe that's what finally did it, havin' some young bloods try to wipe me out.

He set his drink down and made a note in his notebook "Ass kicking by young black nationalists, a turning point."

102

Nawww, that wasn't it, you son of a bitch you! he mumbled fiercely to himself. That wasn't it and you know damned well it wasn't. What's one more ass-kickin', more or less, even if that one put you in the hospital?

He stuck his pen behind his ear and reached for his drink, the city lights seeming to harden into cold, glistening splashes before his eyes.

Lulu's eyes   Lulu's eyes   his bottom woman's eyes gleaming out at him like the eyes of some cursed statue, Lulu's eyes, his dead bottom woman's eyes curled around the hot shot he had accidentally given her as a present.

He poured the rest of the drink down his throat, trying to wash away the memory of the bona fide 'hoe he had been too afraid to love for five years, the one he had pushed, beaten, bullied, slaved, pimped. His bottom lady, the one who had stuck when everybody else had become unglued, the one he had killed.

He pushed the notebook out of his lap and shuffled over to his liquor cabinet for a fresh drink.

And Idella

He shuddered half the glass of scotch down. Idella caught running through the streets, stark ravin' naked, mind completely shot by one-hundred and twenty-six tricks and eight rapes in a day and a half.

And all the rest of them. The poor fools who had come to the big city looking for glamor, romance, finance or whatever the hell it was that they sought and found themselves mummified into whatever Sweet Peter Deeder, pimp extraordinaire, wanted to make of them. He refilled his glass and slouched back over to the sofa, feeling too sad for tears.

Why couldn't I have gotten my ass put in jail for something worthwhile, like Kwendi? Or Buddha? Or gotten killed, like Mayflower? The pantheon of neighborhood figures, sharers at one time of his mystique, flashed through his mind.

He stood up, postured drunkenly, became Ol' Sweet Peter Deeder again, giving commands and making decisions, whippin' asses 'n takin' names.

"Bitch! I thought I told you to bring three-hundred dollars in here! What the fuck am I gon' do with two-ninety-five? What the fuck does this look like to you, Sears' bargain basement?"

"Idella! hold still! Don't you move a fraction of an inch! If you force me to move from this spot when I swing at your motherfuckin' jaw, I'm gon' kill your worthless, triflin', funky, jinky ass! I shoulda exiled your ass to Montana the day after you got here!"

The long, lush nights of being surrounded by soft, loving bodies, the wild flights of fantastic thought, courtesy of Our Girl, Miss Snow, the dynamite weed, the translucent feelings of pure, absolute power.

He settled back onto the sofa, mind juggling the pleasures and horrors of the past. And the remorse, the cold, deep, heart-crumpling awareness of how evil, dumb, foolish and stupid it had been to pimp sisters, black women, his Momma.

A bitter tear swam along the bottom lid of his left eye, threatened to break over the edge, to run down his carefully composed cheek, but failed. He picked up his notebook, put it down, plodded back for another drink and returned to try to get the notes for his new lecture series together.

He sat once again with the notebook in his lap, staring out at the city. Cryptically, he began. "Respect! You can't respect yourself or those you pimp. Nixon had no respect. When I was a pimp, I had no respect. I thought just like him, that everybody was my fool."

He didn't turn when the children rushed into the room, into his work.

"Don't bother Daddy, Tamara! Melba! He's busy!"

Peter Dawson turned to look at his wife, a square-ass high

school teacher with loads of mother wit, a profound understanding of where he had come from, and smiled drunkenly.

She swept the children along in front of her, cold and chattering about their evening at the movies, turning to wink seductively at him as she made her exit, and said, "Don't work all night, Peter   Momma gets cold in bed by herself."

He almost laughed aloud as he scribbled points to make for his next talk, at a co-ed college   thank God! Wonder what kinda 'hoe she woulda made? he mumbled to himself and went on to his next point, feeling tipsy but free.

Chapter 5

Getting By

Lubertha stared at the dull circles under Kwendi's eyes, the heavy, tired, defiant look at the corners of his mouth. Visiting days were much harder sometimes than other times. This was a hard one, Kwendi being out of the Hole for only a week. A feeling that she would never see him again settled in on her, forced words to flow from her.

"We had our first snow this morning."

Kwendi nodded, feeling unable to speak, his love down on him so heavy that he seriously considered jumping across the glass paneled barrier to kiss his woman.

"And, as usual, I found myself wishin' that I was pregnant. I do that a lot, 'specially when it rains or snows."

Kwendi nodded again, realizing that she was writing him a verbal, visiting day letter. Writers are really funny people, he reflected, smiling more now.

"You know, I think the most romantic shit you could ever imagine sometimes. Like, at times I see the two of us floating away, way above the heads of all the people we hate, livin' a really beautiful life."

"Sounds like you're loaded to me," he said softly, humoring her.

She flashed him one of her we-us-you-me smiles. "I guess, at times, in my state of mind I feel naturally high."

Kwendi's mind shot to the middle of his month in solitary. Yeah, you could be high from a lot of things.

"Sometimes I work myself into such a state that I feel, I feel superlucid. Super   ain't it a shame the way people are allowin' this creep to run the government?" she veered off suddenly.

"Uh huh," Kwendi answered quickly, feeling more into the visit second by second. "All of it is just a bunch of drummed up drama. The jive political drama. Well, we know where that takes us . . . hah! there's got to be somethin' better than the Republicans 'n the Democrats. The sociological drummed up drama, hyped up social divisions that make it supereasy to keep the real rulers, the money grubbers, in power.

"Ooops, I'm sorry, baby," he apologized, "I didn't mean to monopolize the conversation. How's your father?"

"Oh, that's o.k., I get off into things myself, as you well know. Daddy's become such a groove. The other night he came home growlin', with a newspaper under his arm, spread it out on the kitchen table and actually started ravin'! I mean, sho' nuff ravin'!"

"What about?" Kwendi asked quickly, the contagious feeling of something seriously funny making him feel that way.

"Something we had rapped about a few nights before, he 'n I, Manipulation by Big Money Interests. I can't remember exactly what the article was sayin', but at any rate, in its

108

own shabby way, it was tryin' to justify jackin' up the poor so that the rich could get some more."

"I can dig it."

"Anyway, I don't know about my Daddy sometimes, he can come off with the weirdest notions in the world sometimes. Especially about politics, but what I've been noticing more and more, is that he'll come right back at me with my argument a week later, if necessary."

Kwendi laughed, seeing Mr. Franklin's brusque manner and his bristling mustache in his mind's eye. "When's your book comin' out?" he veered off, anxious now to ask, say everything, knowing that the visit would be over too soon.

"Ohh, 'bout the first of the year," she replied, trying to be modest. "You know, even though Third World Press is publishing it, they still want to take advantage of the commercial side of things. Can you imagine, Kwendi ...? I got a book comin' out, about us! What more could any writer ask for?"

"Well, since it's about the Struggle, let's hope it gets read," he stated drily.

"Yeah, me too," she said wistfully, "Kwendi! guess what happened the other day?"

"No, what!!?" he responded gleefully, playing out a little number on her spontaneous bursts.

"The Negroes for a Latter Day Hitler, or whatever the name of the organization is, came to us, to talk about funding our theater group. Their only stipulation was that we would 'tone' down the messages in our work. Can you imagine what kind of souls those niggers must have, in order to be able to make up the words to ask us to do something like that? Especially in these times."

"Well, hey, baby   you know, it just doesn't register with a lot of sisters 'n brothers that we are now living in a fascist state, a Neo-New World fascist state, but still a fascist state.

109

Yeahhh, it really is hard to try to figure out where people are coming from, at times," he concluded sadly.

The guard stood at Kwendi's left shoulder, not saying a word, as though he were eavesdropping and overseeing at the same time. Lubertha saw the muscles tighten in Kwendi's jaws as the guard casually tapped him on the shoulder.

"Awright, Jones   it's time."

Kwendi half turned toward the guard. It's time ... for you, that means ending the only pleasure I have these days, my woman visiting me. It's time   what do you know about time?

"Be cool, Kwendi," Lubertha whispered urgently to him. "Be cool, baby."

He relaxed and stood, gave her a soulful look and turned away with the guard grasping his elbow, unnecessarily.

She sat there, as she had done a number of times after a visit, feeling rotten, suddenly remembering the little things she had wanted to tell him but could never seem to remember.

Sweet Peter Deeder, Peter Dawson, reformed pimp, offering to make some fund raising speeches for the Club.

I've stopped smoking   so much anyway.

Kwendi. Five years without Kwendi. Five hurtin' years. No deep kisses, no picnics in the park, movies, no jazz concerts, dances, parties. Is the Cause worth it? she asked herself, glancing up and down the row of convict faces on the other side of the glass paneled visitor's glass.

A couple of the black inmates raised their fists in her direction, a toast for black liberation, recognizing that she was Kwendi's woman.

She smiled back weakly, drained.

Yeah, the Cause is worth it. She slid out of the seat and strolled slowly out of the visitor's section, her mind suddenly swamped by the amount of Club business she had to take care of. Oh well, at least it's Monday, that does give me the rest of the week.

Big Momma bustled around her room, pouring a little more tea from her twenty-one year old teapot, into the sister's cups, her arthritic knees aching slightly. "I'll be with y'all in just a few minutes, ladies," she said, resettling the teapot on her two burner, and disappeared behind the Chinese screen in her room to change.

"Take your time, sister," one of the Muslim sisters spoke out in a clear, deep voice.

Mrs. Washington struggled nervously with the buttons on her washed out gingham dress, fumbling out of her old cardigan at the same time, bursitis adding to the effort. She peeked through a slit in the screen at the two sisters, both of them close to her age, straight gowns and headgear making them look somehow like ... her mind fumbled for the right image

like ol' time Egyptian queens. And the way they sit ... so straight. Her heart pounded from unaccustomed excitement. This was her fifth trip to the mosque, courtesy of Baby ... Lawwd! when am I gon' ever remember that child's other name? Robert 30X!

The first couple trips had been made out of boredom mostly, and in response to the many kindnesses Robert had shown her as the hard wintertime settled in   bringing bags of groceries ("Sorry, Sister Washington, no pork chops in this sack") and warm sweaters, all donated by the Sisterhood. The first few trips had been kind of funny. They had sent two sisters over to escort her, and she had felt compelled to go. The mosque itself had struck her in an odd way, what with the quiet and the efficiency, no bustling Christianity anywhere around, meaning bullshit. But most of all, the extremely polite way all of the visitors had been treated.

And especially the older folks, she reflected, meaning me. She reached up into the closet behind her for a purse thinking back to the nice feeling she had gotten from being around women her own age, several of them ex-Baptists, who walked proudly, seemed to have no ol' aches and pains and gave all the credit for lack of afflictions to being followers of the Honorable Elijah Muhammed. It was almost like being down home when young folks respected gray hair, didn't give grown-ups no backtalk and people acted like they had some sense or a place to be.

At any rate, it sure as hell beat sittin' up in the window, day in and day out, trying to be interested in everybody else's life.

She peeked back through the slit at the two sisters, her overshoes, cloth coat and bird feathered hat on, purse hanging on her throbbing arm. They look so at peace with theyselves, just sittin', seemin' to not be worried about a daggoned thang.

She stood back from the screen, her lips pursed, thinking, considering. They don't drink. Well, that ain't no problem for me, I only used to drink that moonshine with Booker when he was alive ... Lawd Bless his soul! Cain't eat the pig. Well, the way prices is these days, that would be a savin'.

She swept through all the rules and regulations for a good Muslim life that she had listened to at the meetings, soft-sell orientation sessions, and found herself in tune with them; if nothing else they offered her the peace and security an old woman needed after her youth had been spent struggling to survive a life in the big city.

She took a hesitant step from behind the screen, her mind suddenly focusing on one thing. If I joined up, could I still dip snuff?! She took a deep, hard look at the Muslim sisters who had come for her, standing respectfully, waiting for her to announce that they could leave.

Who in the hell cared about whether or not you could dip some damned snuff!?   with a new life waiting.

"I'm ready   sisters   we can go now."

112

They beamed at her as she walked toward them, her knees aching a little less, knowing that Allah, the All Gracious, the Most Merciful, had revived another lost soul.

"Watch 'em, Phyllisine!" Hattie Evans whispered to her daughter as she went behind the meat counter to wait on Miss Rabbit.

Phyllisine's eyes followed her mother's broad hips as she waddled away. Watch who?? Lil' ol' Andy Johnson and Marsha Kelly? They weren't even tall enough to steal anything, and if they did, the most it could be would be a cupcake or a piece of bubble gum.

She scorned the thought of being so petty, glanced out at Big Momma whisking by in a car load of Muslim sisters ... hmmmm   looks like they finally convinced her   and heard her mother ask, in that jive tone of voice that sounded so superphoney to her ears, as though she were the head waitress in some swank restaurant, "And what can I do for you today, Miss Rabbit?"

"Wellllll," she heard Miss Rabbit begin, in her heavy contralto, "I was thinkin' 'bout buyin' some halonnis, but seein' how it's so high, I don't know," and then went off into that mumbling study period that so many of their customers spent time in these days.

She smiled warmly over the counter at lil' Andy and Marsha, eight and nine respectively, window shopping with options on buying, twelve cents between them.

Phyllisine's eyes darted from her mother's studied cool behind the meat counter, back to Marsha and Andy, looking furtively at her as they wandered up one aisle and down the other one, noses snotty. She beckoned to them, on the q.t. They responded, ghetto hip, like, who? me? pointing at their chests with their eyes.

Yeahhh, you! she answered with her own set of visual

113

signals and watched them approach the counter with deep love, strong feeling for their reluctance, like knowing they'd gone through the "we've-had-firecrackers-tied-to-our-tails" syndrome.

"Mmmmmm," Miss Rabbit's hum of price consideration reached her from across the store, "since I don't see anything in here that costs less than the 'lonni, I guess I'll have to settle for a quarter pound o' that. Uhhh, Hattie, while I'm about it, you got any scraps I can feed my lil' ol' dog?"

"Whatchu got in mind, Miss Rabbit?" she heard her mother ask in a monotone, mindful of the fact that Miss Rabbit didn't have a dog, and never did have one.

"Oooohh, I don't know, some o' that fat meat that y'all throw away, that you cain't sell."

Phyllisine glanced quickly in her mother's direction to make certain that she wasn't watching, and reached over the counter with an oatmeal cookie in each hand. Andy and Marsha snapped them out of her hands like hungry dogs, aware, instantly into what she was doing. Their hurried looks toward her mother bending behind the meat counter, dealing with Miss Rabbit's needs, said thank you.

She remounted the high stool behind the cash register, smiling at Andy and Marsha's low profiled exit.

Mrs. Evans glanced up from slicing a quarter of a pound of bologna for Miss Rabbit to see the two children leave the store, theftless to her point of view, looking at their backs.

Phyllisine reassured her with a nod that everything was cool. Mrs. Evans kept on slicing bologna, giving Miss Rabbit an extra piece of the thinly sliced meat.

"That'll be forty-six cents, Miss Rabbit."

"Forty-six cents!?" Miss Rabbit reacted, peering up at the scale, unable to read it, but peering up at it anyway.

"Forty-six cents," Phyllisine heard her mother announce in a familiar dry monotone.

"Wellll," Miss Rabbit finally sighhhhed, "I guess if it's forty-six cents, it's forty-six cents."

"It's forty-six cents," Mrs. Evans replied, wrapping the ersatz meat up in a piece of yesterday's newspaper . . .

"Uhhh, Hattie, what about those scraps?" Miss Rabbit pressed.

"I'll look 'n see what I got," Mrs. Evans answered, annoyance creeping into her voice.

Phyllisine watched her mother pass the small package to Miss Rabbit, grease penciled 46¢, and saw her bend down to pick through the fatty scraps with a pinch of meat attached.

"Thank you, thank you very much, Sister Evans," Miss Rabbit said as she accepted the additional newspaper wrapped scraps and wandered over to pay Phyllisine for her purchase.

Phyllisine took the purchase and the gift of fat and dropped them both into a small brown bag, her stomach churning from feelings she couldn't really come to grips with. A lot of people were asking for scraps these days. She knew it would have been much more possible to get scraps with real hunks of meat on them from the big supermarkets . . . but who asked them for anything? And how many forms would you have to fill out to get it?

Miss Rabbit slid a weather-beaten dollar bill across the counter at her, smiling in her semi-toothless, graceful fashion. Phyllisine took her money, rang up the sale, gave her change and stared with dead eyes as she slouched past the potato bin and swiped a potato.

Right on, sister! she screamed silently to her, the words making a raggedy sound in her consciousness as Rudy Little strode into the store past Miss Rabbit.

Mrs. Evans looked up from behind the meat counter to see who it was, checked Rudy out, decided his expression was non-larcenous, went back to arranging the three day old meat in front of the two day old meat.

115

Rudy glanced furtively at Mrs. Evans' darting hands in the meat display counter and laid a note on the counter in front of Phyllisine.

They both stared at it for a few seconds, she because he had placed it there, puzzling her, and he because he suddenly felt very self-conscious, wondering if he was doing the right thing. She looked at him curiously, unfolded the note and read it in a couple quick glances. And then again, slowly. "I've been wanting to take you out for quite awhile, but I've hesitated to ask you for many reasons. Can you go to the show with me Saturday night?"

Phyllisine looked into Rudy's steady brown-eyed gaze and nodded yes, folding the note into her fist. Yes, she nodded again, to make certain he understood.

"Seven-thirty," he said quietly, "in front of the liquor store."

She agreed silently with another nod, as he casually strolled out of the store.

"What did he want?" her mother asked, waddling over to check out the evening's receipts before her ol' man came downstairs.

"Oh," Phyllisine thought quickly, "he wanted some cigarettes, one o' those foreign brands, Galouses or something like that."

"Hmf! That's the trouble with them semi-educated niggers, they always wantin' something we don't stock."

Phyllisine smiled slightly, faking agreement, moved aside to let her mother get to the register, the note clutched tightly in her balled up fist.

Seven-thirty Saturday night, the movies with Rudy Little, law student, one of the neighborhood's shining lights. Maybe I should've cooled myself out a bit, she thought . . . but shit! What purpose would that have served?

Miss Rabbit washed the scraps of meat in a pot of hot water, twice   pared off as much of the fat from the lean as possible and set the pot of water with the manicured scraps onto a low fire. She stood with her hands braced on her hips for a few minutes, looking down into the pot of scraps, her brow knitted with deep thoughts.

Tonight

Steam began to rise from the slowly bubbling fatty tissue in the pot before she shuffled away to pull an onion and a potato out of a sack in her kitchen cabinet. She sliced the onion up into the pot, diced the potato and salted and peppered the mixture and stood, as before, staring deeply into the pot.

She held both her hands out in front of her, the short butcher knife trembling slightly in her left hand. She lowered her hands slowly, covered the pot, placed the knife on the kitchen table and strolled from the kitchen to look out of her front window, restlessly.

Her eyes swept up and down the street, taking everything in   Lubertha's writing lamp across the street from her, Big Momma's shades drawn, a young man urinating through the burglar guard mesh drawn across the front of ol' man Jackson's store, Rudy Little hurrying up the street with a load of books under his arm, coming from the library, Bessie Mae and Fred Lee coming from somewhere. She smiled affectionately at them.

A light, dirty snow blanketing the whole scene. The police cruising through the neighborhood with their headlights dimmed.

She eased away from the window with a sigh and walked back to the kitchen, feeling very old and unusually tired. Oh Lawwwd, ha'mercy, she mumbled aloud and folded her arms across her breasts. Lawd in Heaven, please give me the strength.

The knocks were so soft that she thought for a second that

117

it might be the sound of something other than someone at the back door. And then, again.

"Yesss, who is it?"

"Lena," a soft voice answered.

Miss Rabbit opened the back door just enough for her to slip through. Both women avoided looking into each other's faces.

"Kinda nippy out there, ain't it?" Miss Rabbit commented, attempting to cool the tension out.

Lena nodded stiffly and slowly pulled her head scarf off. They stood in the center of the kitchen floor, uncomfortably.

"You bring the kotex?" Miss Rabbit asked quietly, professionally.

Lena nodded numbly and held up a brown paper bag.

"You all washed up 'n everything?" Miss Rabbit probed gently.

Lena nodded again, not trusting her voice, and leaned slightly toward Miss Rabbit's shoulder.

The older woman embraced her, calming her. "Don't worry, honey   everythin' gon' be awright. Why don't we sit 'n have a cuppa coffee? Here, lemme take your coat."

Lena shook her arms out of her cloth coat, moving as though she were in a hypnotic trance. Miss Rabbit seated her at the kitchen table, placed a large pot of water on the back burner, stirred her "stew" a few times and quickly heated a small sauce pan of water for instant coffee.

"Sorry, honey," she apologized, "but I ain't got no cream."

Lena smiled shyly, accepting the cup. "That's awright, I like it black, with just a lil' sugar."

Miss Rabbit sat across from her, consciously straightening her back to inspire confidence.

Lena took a few nervous sips of coffee. "Will it hurt?" she asked suddenly.

Miss Rabbit slowly lowered her cup, deliberately placed

118

it on the table with studied strength and shook her head, "No, not much, but it ain't gon' feel good as it felt makin' it." She surreptitiously checked out the steamy fog forming over the boiling pot of water on the back burner.

"Matter of fact, we may as well gon' 'n git it over with."

"What do I have to do?" Lena asked, swallowing the words fearfully.

"Well, first thang is to help me clear the table."

"This table?!"

"Uhhn huh, the light in here is better than it is anywhere else in the house."

Lena obediently removed the coffee cups.

"Wash it off real good," Miss Rabbit instructed her as she strode away to her bedroom, heart beating like a drum. "There's some cleanser in the window over the sink."

She knelt quickly by the side of her bed, underneath the Anglo Jesus with the celestially visible heart, and prayed fervently, profoundly. "O sweet Jesus, please grant me the strength to help this young woman out. Dear Lawd, please let my hand be strong 'n true, please dear God, I pray to you."

She struggled to her feet and reached over to her knitting basket. She inspected the sharp points of two of the needles to make certain that there was no material attached to them, snatched her pillow from the bed and pulled a clean sheet out of the dresser drawer. She almost burst into tears as she walked back into the kitchen to find Lena staring at the table as though it were a slab in the city morgue.

"Did you wash it good?" she asked sharply, masking her feelings.

"Uh huh."

"Good. Now here, help me."

The two women moved slowly, covering the table with the sheet as though they were performing a ritual. Miss Rabbit placed the pillow at one end and two chairs, stirrup style,

119

at both sides of the table at the other end. Efficiently, she checked the back door lock, made certain that the shades were drawn and came finally to stand in front of Lena.

"Now you have to lay up here, Lena 'n spread your legs, just like you was gon' have a baby, in order for me to do what I got to do. But first, lemme ask you again, are you sho' you don't want to have this ...?"

A slow trickle of tears slid down Lena Daniels' high cheekbones as she lay on the table. "Yes, yes I want to have the baby, but we can't afford it, Miss Rabbit we can hardly feed the ones we got."

Miss Rabbit patted her on the arm, "I understand, sweetheart, I understand. Awright now, sit up first you gon' have to take off your clothes, go on, undress. I'll git one of my ol' flannel gowns for you to put on."

She watched Lena unbutton the first three buttons of her blouse, sadly, deeply into her reluctant feelings. Oh God, she prayed, walking back to her bedroom for the gown Oh God, please help me, help us She fished the gown out and reacted with intense surprise to see the glistening, naked young woman in her kitchen, standing under the light, next to the white sheeted table.

"Here ya go, put this on," she said kindly and began to review her procedure, her equipment. Boil needle tips, have kotex ready for possible hemorrhage, and, oh yes that.

"Lena Mae, you ain't hardly got stretchmark the first, how'd you manage that?"

Lena laughed easily for the first time, "I don't know, Jim says crumbcrushers just squirt outta me, don't need no stretchin'."

Miss Rabbit rinsed one of the coffee cups out and circled Lena sitting stoically on the edge of the table, Miss Rabbit's old-fashioned flannel nightie molding her full figure. She reached to the top shelf of her kitchen cabinet, over behind

120

a few cans of reserve soup and some dried beans for two small tea-packaged sized bags, poured a few careful measures from each of the bags into the cup.

Lena, resigned to it all, peered curiously at her back. "Can I help you with anything, Miss Rabbit?"

"No, honey, not really," she replied, feeling strong and positive in her actions now, on home ground. She replaced the bags, bustled over to whip some hot water into the cup, poured two teaspoons of salt into it behind the hot water and stirred vigorously.

"Now Lena," she said, blowing into the steaming cup, "I want you to drink this, as hot as you can bear it."

"What is . . .?"

"Just do like I say, girl! 'n stop askin' so many questions!" she snapped, her nerves on edge. She left her pursing her lips up to sip at the steaming brew and went about the business of sterilizing her needles.

"How's it goin'?" she asked without turning around.

"It's hot and it tastes turrible," Lena replied between shudders.

Miss Rabbit smiled, remembering. "Drink much as you can of it! Push it down, don't throw up." The needles sterilized, she turned to face Lena with a firm set of her jaw.

"Now this is your last chance, do you want to . . .?"

Lena tilted the cup up and drank, scalding her mouth as the liquid ran down, a cold, resolved expression on her face.

Miss Rabbit said one more silent prayer as Lena placed her feet evenly in each stirrup chair, pulled the bottom of the gown up over her face and submissively lowered her head to the pillow.

Miss Rabbit blinked at the sight of the strongly muscled young black thighs spread, the small, gashed wound between. Beads of sweat suddenly popped out on her forehead as she eased up between Lena's legs with the needles, remembering when they used to use cobwebs and soot to stop bleeding.

She smelled the odor at the end of the operation, suddenly realized that she had boiled her meal to death and said to Lena, crying convulsively under her nightgown veil. "Hush up woman! Stop that cryin'! You ain't done nothin' but lose an unwanted mouth, I done burned my stew!"

Lena uncovered her tear-streaked face and smiled at Miss Rabbit's nitty gritty logic.

Lubertha shuffled her notes, trying to maintain a cool exterior as the arguments escalated on both sides of her, the final result of internal dissensions that had been brewing quietly but powerfully since the late summer and now, during the fourth week of the new year, were spilling out. The Club membership was facing The Year of The Tiger with bristling fangs.

Ojenkasi made his voice heard above the general noise, "Abdul! Chiyo! Maisha! All of you sisters 'n brothers, listen to me a minute!"

The group quieted down slightly, granting attention to a senior member.

"I don't think that what y'all want to git off into would suit the spirit of what Kwendi is all about, the kinds of things we could accomplish his way," he spoke with quiet passion, a pained look on his face.

"Kwendi's in jail, man!" Abdul, his full beard bristling up aggressively, "and besides, who in the fuck are you to be tryin' to tell us what the dude is all about?! There his woman sit, if anybody could tell us anything 'bout where he's comin' from, it would be her, not you!"

All eyes in the room suddenly swept to Lubertha, as though suddenly remembering that she was there.

She stacked her notes slowly, neatly, all of her enlightening points seemingly pointless now, and looked around the

122

room at the faces she had grown up with, suffered with, loved.

No, no talk about the government's jive economic policies tonight, the price of beans in the ghetto, and why. No intelligent, well thought out ideas on ways to improve Afro-American, Pan-African unity or any of the other points. This went deeper than all that, this was soul searching time.

"O.k., number one," she began, her voice trembling slightly. "I know that some o' y'all are gonna think that I've either lost my mind, gone crazy, or both. I don't give a damn, one way or the other. I'm gon' say what I righteously feel."

"Go 'head, sister!" Ojenkasi encouraged her, his jaw muscles twitching.

"Everybody in here knows that Kwendi Jones is my life, and that my life is locked up."

Maisha, Nici and Bobbi looked down at their feet sadly.

"But that doesn't mean, under any circumstances, that we haven't been free with each other. There're times when I get letters from Kwendi or I go to see him, and it seems that he has much more of his shit together than any of us out here in the streets."

Chiyo grumbled deep down in his throat, annoyed with her obliqueness.

"All I can do is ask you all to be patient with me," she shot at him, a fierce look in her eyes. "I'm not gon' suddenly start talkin' like a goddamned computer!"

"Right on, sister!" Abdul, a dissenter agreed, and glared at Chiyo.

"Now then," her voice gained force, "let's go back a lil' bit, to reaffirm where the organization, the Club was supposed to be goin'."

A few of the younger members and some of the oldsters leaned forward, having fallen out of pocket for the real reason for their existence in the Club.

"In the beginning, almost five years ago now, as *some* of

123

you remember, we started out as a creative writin' group, a *revolutionary* group that was dedicated to exposin', within our community, the total community, all of the sham and bullshit we could write about and change, by any means necessary. In the beginning, we screened people very closely to see where their heads were, but Kwendi, from a prison cell, said 'Hey y'all! that's too goddamned elitist! If a sister or a brother wants to be in, they ought to be allowed in, period.' We didn't deal with white folks comin' into the Club because we weren't concerned with white folks' rights .. and we still ain'."

A few members of the audience seconded her comments with "Right-ons!!"

Lubertha paused, pushed her notes aside, "The Club, even from the beginnin', despite the fact that we were pro-black, was never anti-white, not on the person to person level. Am I right about that, Johnny?"

Johnny Fox, his arms crossed, analyzing as usual, nodded in agreement.

"We considered the possibilities, at one time, of a few selective murders," she went on coldly, "within the white community, if it would serve a positive purpose for black people. But, because of our intelligence at that time" she fixed her look on Abdul   "we decided against that,

and I'm sure Brother Tucker can open up the book and back me up on these points. We decided to attack the oppressor on all fronts, short of murder, which is what I hear now.

"Pleazzzz," she almost moaned the word, "please don't nobody get the impression that I'm against the idea of killin' a few pigs who've tried to make our lives miserable   but where do you stop? I mean, do we go from there to dynamitin' police stations? Assassinating politicians who aren't doin' what they should be doin' for the people, black and white . . .?

124

"Nawwww, nawwww, that's not where I want to go," she waved her hands in exasperation. "I don't want to get bogged down with this localized oppression we've always been programmed to deal with. I want to branch out, form a Club bond with oppressed people everywhere, deal with the shit that's threatenin' to wipe all poor people out."

"Speak, sister!" BoBo called out, looking self-consciously at Abdul and Chiyo.

She smiled at him gratefully, feeling slightly confused about where her spontaneous speech was going. "Look, everybody I'd just like to rap for a few more minutes, and then I'll give it up."

"Go 'head, blow!" Ojenkasi spoke coldly at her side.

"I got a letter from Kwendi the other day that laid so much shit on my mind that I had to take a couple aspirin."

"Hahhh hahhh hahhah!"

"Right on!"

"Brother, don't be jivin'!"

"Y'all wanna know what he said?"

"If you don't tell us," Nici Miles cut in humorously, "I'm gon' kick yo' ass!"

Lubertha laughed, the mood of things lightening somewhat. "To begin with, it was a love letter, but I'll skip that part of it. What he got into was what he felt was the fascist thang a lot of brothers 'n sisters were gettin' into. He started talkin' about how important it was to have unity, but not unity with absolute conformity, which is where some of us want to take things. Abdul says, if we don't want to go out and shoot pigs or pour gasoline on white women 'n kids, then we ain't ready. I have to disagree with him . . . ."

Abdul scowled at her, biting his bottom lip.

"I don't think we have to sink to the subhuman level that the white boy has let his technology take him to, in dealin' with people, in order to get our human rights. I know it's

125

necessary for black people to do a whole bunch o' things, but I don't think any of our methods should be applied to individuals   Racism is an institution, not a person."

Abdul stood slowly, his scowl deepening. "Sister Franklin, with all due respect. We went through all this shit a few years back, and we came to the realization that the only way, *the only way!* we gon' get rid of white oppression, in all its forms, the only way we gon' be granted more than a token share of what this country has gained at the sacrifice of our lives 'n labor is through bloodshed 'n violence.

"Now, you know yourself," he added suavely, "this is one of the things Kwendi was really heavy on."

Lubertha wiped her face with both hands, frustrated, disturbed. "Abdul, that was almost five years ago. Many, many things've changed, some for the better, some for the worse. Five years ago that cracker governor, the one in Alabama, whatshisname? was a superduper white racist, o.k.? Now, most of his shit has changed.

"Five years ago we had to deal with forces that were not the least bit ready to deal with any of the places we were comin' from. Times've changed, and times are changin', brother   whether we like to admit it or not. The racists we knew as children have given birth to children who are not racists. We can't afford to be stuck with old methods dealin' with new people."

"Bullshit!" Chiyo Mungu called out. "How in the fuck can a beast give birth to anything but a beast!?"

"I don't know, brother," she answered promptly, not stuttering over a single syllable. "I don't know the answer to that. But, it's just as hard to figure out how slaves could give birth to free men. Mutations come in many colors."

A few members of the audience applauded, giving credit to an evenly placed point.

"The only thing I'm sayin'," Lubertha continued, on firmer

126

footing now, "is this; I don't think we should be guilty of committin' the same mistakes that the white racists committed, in the name of freedom. When I sit here and listen to Abdul say that we ought to go out in small groups and kill a few whiteys, *any* few   then I feel we've gone off and become white ourselves."

"What!?" Chiyo screamed. "What's that you say?"

"You heard me, brother   I didn't bite my tongue. When I hear you say that we should start a war that we sho' in hell ain't in no shape to win, in order to stop war   then I call that traditional white thinkin'. You dig? Like, hey, we had to destroy your house in order to keep the enemy away. Who is the enemy?"

She paused for a quick breath and jammed on, cutting off Cyiyo, Abdul and a few others who wanted to dispute her. "This is the kind of thinkin' that we must *not* fall into, I am not tryin' to preach the philosophy of St. Martin Luther King either, all I'm tryin' to do is make sense.

"One of the reasons why we have Rudy in law school, why we raked and scraped enough dough together to send him, was to have a lawyer, one who would attempt to deal with the law from our perspective for a change. That's called doin' something by any means necessary too, you know?

"If y'all remember, when we first got active on the political scene, a lot of people called us sellouts and a bunch of other foul things, but look at what happened when the neighborhood began to benefit from what we were into."

"Why don't you give somebody else a chance to speak, sister? That's what's wrong now, the same people always have the flo'!"

Lubertha glared across the room at Chico Daddy, a red, black and green knit stuffed down onto his braided curls. Chico Daddy, the one dude in the group who never said very much. Maybe he's right, she thought, and sat down without

127

saying another word.

The room was suddenly alive with crosscurrents, Abdul on top of the main one.

He eased into his thing suavely, confident that a certain number would dig him as a man, rather than any woman, and that a certain number would dig him because he was there, alive, in the flesh, and their so-called leader wasn't. "Sister speaks well, yeahhh, sister speaks well, but we have to consider a lot of other things besides what she says. We have to keep in mind the nature of the beast we dealin' with. Number one   he's the same devil with thirty-two fangs that he was when he first slithered out from under that rock whenever that was."

"Right on, brother! right on!"

"Git down!" and some other admiring, exclamatory remarks backed up Abdul's opening.

Lubertha smiled sadly, becoming aware that it had all been planned. It was obvious that Abdul had been picked for the confrontation and probably the leadership. But why?

"I know," he went on, sounding more like a new line Black Baptist preacher all the time, "I know that what the sister says is true. Yeah! The Club has done a lot! But what I'm sayin' is that we should be doin' more! more! more of everything!

"If it takes blowin' away a few of the pigs, then those who got chicken hearts should stand back with the women 'n children!" He glared pointedly at Ojenkasi. Ojenkasi, confident of his manhood, shook his head and smirked disdainfully.

The group followed the scene, bursting with unh-huhs and right-ons! and other comments designed to let the speaker know that he was being given their attention.

"I'm not gon' bite my tongue to say it, I think we've been slippin' toward a too soft, too sweet thang for too long. An organization like ours has to remain tough 'n hard, bitter to

128

the roots!"

"That's what's wrong with a lotta brothers like you, Abdul!" Ojenkasi cut in, unable to be cool any longer. "You dudes have such a helluva vested interest in the bitter section of things that you can't even get ready for anything sweet."

"You say that to say what?" Abdul asked, sarcasm melting over each word.

"Take it for what it's worth. I know, you know and damned near everybody with any sense knows that the shit here ain't near 'bout right! Not by a long shot! But what you remind me of is the dude who's been complainin' all his motherfuckin' life about one thing or the other, and when he gets it squared away, he keeps on complainin' 'cause that's all he knows how to do."

"See! See what I'm talkin' about!" Abdul jabbed his finger at Ojenkasi, giving his followers and would-be followers a focal point. "That's one of the things wrong in here,   that jiveass, superduper, intellectual bullshit! The minute one of us starts talkin' about doin' instead of talkin', we get twisted back around the stick with a bunch o' words.

"We wants some action! Damn these proverbs and stinky, pootbutt pacifist ideas! Action, brotherman! Action is what we need! Direct, coldblooded action!"

Lubertha, in the middle of the discussion, quietly stuffed her notes into her purse, her mind already dealing with the sad letter she would have to write Kwendi, and stood up to leave.

The room was silenced by her movement.

"Hey, don't stop arguin' 'n squabblin' for my benefit, just because I'm leavin'. Keep it up, maybe some good will come of it. I sure in hell hope so."

Tears wobbled around in the corner of her eyes, threatening to spill out. "I don't have anything bad to say about or to anybody here, nobody knows better than I do what frustration will make you do. I can't really make myself feel the way Abdul feels, or Chiyo or Kwendi or anybody else because everybody comes from a slightly different place in their heads.

"All I can say is this, I understand. As a black woman, as a black American human being, I understand."

She strolled down the aisle to the exit, nodding to the people she felt close to. They nodded back, knowing that she had dismissed herself.

She closed the door behind her softly, stood on the outside leaning against it for a minute or two, listening to the shocked silence and then to the furious sounds of ten different debates.

God! she whispered to the shadows   what will it take to get black people really and truly together, some kind of way?

Lucille stared out at the darkness absently, tired. "And then what did he say?" she asked politely, glancing at the sight of Lubertha stumbling down the street. Looks like she's been drinking.

"Nothin', that was it. You know how it is, they don't really wanna rehire me no way, at my age, with a bad back. If it wasn't for the union, they woulda fired me the day I got hurt."

Lucille Smith stirred her spoon around slowly in her luke-warm coffee, worn down from doing Mrs. Bernhammer's housework, mind half on her husband's problems with getting back to work, receiving retroactive compensation, a foul-up, courtesy of Ms. Swartz, and coercing a reluctant company doctor to grant him a medical clearance. The other part of her consciousness dealt with more prosaic hardships the bills piling up, the rent due, Mrs. Bernhammer, hip to her problems, becoming snottier every day, making up for all the independent retorts she had received from her "house-worker" in the past.

"Aren't you finished with the furniture polishing yet, Mrs.

130

Smith?"

"If I had four hands I'd be finished by now."

"Maybe age is slowing you up, Mrs. Smith."

Fergy looked down at his hands circling the coffee cup and felt worthless, helpless. What a helluva way to tie a man up. They tell you that you're able to go back to work, but ineligible. They say that you need a clearance to go back to work and the only one who can grant it, the only one, is the company's doctor, who doesn't want to see you go back. And if that ain't enough, there's the goddamned Industrial Accident Board and that crock-minded bitch handlin' the case, Mzzz. FuckitupSwartz.

He looked up from the cup into his woman's face.

Damn she looks tired.

He reached over to stroke her hands.

"Don't worry, baby   we gon' work it out somehow."

She looked down at her man's hands, so strong   and felt a little less tired. "Fergy, I ain't worried 'bout a gotdamned thing!" she spoke out with sudden energy and started clearing the table. "This ain't the first time we been shot through the grease, 'n it probably won't be the last time."

He slouched in his chair, watching his woman's hips shimmy slightly as she rinsed their coffee cups out, the movement accentuated by her glistening nylon nightie.

She turned to him suddenly. "Fergy, did you take your medicine tonight?"

He uncoiled himself from his seat and walked over to embrace her. "Nawwww, I didn't take it, and I ain't gon' take it tonight."

"Why not?" she asked, halfway between honest curiosity and middle-aged coyness.

" 'Cause they put me right t' sleep, and I don't feel like goin' right t' sleep tonight," he replied purposefully and kissed her flush on the mouth, tenderly.

131

Chapter 6
Midweek Changes

Kanoon looked deeply into the almond shaped eyes of the tall, dark skinned woman standing under the exit sign with him at the front door of the Pot.

"Why can't I spend the night, Kanoon?" he heard her ask through his cocaine, music soaked fog.

" 'Cause like I told you, baby .. I don't like to spend the whole night with nobody, they think they own you when they spend the night."

The woman looked out sadly at the cold streets beyond the large, black-painted picture window, and all around herself at the uptilted stools and tables of the club.

"You sho' is cold, Kanoon," she said quietly.

He shrugged eloquently, denying nothing.

She leaned her lush pelvis into him and smoothly draped

her arms around his slender shoulders. "Why can't I stay a lil' while longer?" she cooed into his ear, a fountain of promises in the question.

"Number one, 'cause I don't want no mo', and number two 'cause I got some work to do."

She withdrew her arms and stood back to take his full measure, eyes narrowed, hands on hips. "You know, they told me when I first got on the scene that you were a heartless, cold-blooded lil' motherfucker, but I didn't know you were this . . . ."

Kanoon unlocked the door and stood beside it like a Prussian doorman, impatient for his latest guest to depart. "Good night, Justine."

She smiled a cool little smile at him as she stepped through the door into the cold air of the pumpkin hour. "Goodnight, Kanoon," she replied, giving up, and leaned back to kiss him once again.

"Be careful goin' to your car, baby," he cautioned her. "We got lotsa high crime rates hangin' 'round out there."

She laid a dazzling, sarcastic smile over her shoulder at him as she clutched her fur to her throat and tripped to the gun metal painted Porsche at the curb.

He stood in the doorway, freezing in his paisley caftan, and watched her zip away over patches of ice and tainted snow. He closed the door, carefully rebolted it and strolled around the empty club aimlessly for a minute, winding up finally seated on the apron of the stage.

The Pot, my club, he bragged to himself, my club, no grubby white hands anywhere in the Pot. Funny, he smiled in the dim light, how many different ideas circulate about how I wound up with this place. Some bitch got it for me. The Mafia owns it. So and so own a piece. I bet all them motherfuckers would shit a brick if they knew that my talk is fo' real, it's all mines. Yeahhh

He sprawled back on the stage, laced his hands under his grimly tattered naps and stared up at the light fixtures in the ceiling for five thoughtful minutes.

Justine, Nancy, Luella, Mercedes, Donyale, Branille, Hora, Tamu, Cleo, Margarite, Shirlean, Flavia, Maureen, Darcye, Susan, Janice, Loretta, Nicca, Graciela, Toshiko, La Na, Amy, Melba, Eartha, Katherine, Margo, Joan, Yellow Bird-eyes, Roberta, Lois, Coco, Azul, Otani, Nina, Freda, Francine, Le Noir, Phyllis, Georgina, Wilhelmina, Norma, Clotilde, Ingrid, Anouk, Jo Jo, Alice, Mozella, Madeline, Jakki, Lady, Bop Girl, Stella, Barbara, Sheryl, Veronica, Daisy, Pashalusta, Maisha, Naima, Aissa,   Aissa . . . Aissa . . . .

He cut off the litany of females he had slept with over the course of the last two years, those that had made an impression on him, by sitting up.

Damn! he mumbled, feeling the weight of his stiffened penis against his thigh. Damn! I should've let that bitch stay.

He sat up straighter, trying to force his erection away Jacqueleen, Carla, Pamela, Francesca, Natalia, Nira . . . discovered that it wasn't going to happen as long as his memory continued functioning sensually, walked over to the bar, the front of his caftan jutting out like a Greek spear.

He looked up into the mirror behind the bar as he walked toward it, caught sight of the thumb piano beckoning to him from a chair on the bandstand. Yeahhhhh   he spoke to the instrument and himself as he did an about face and hopped onto the stand.

He stood looking down at the small, half-kidney shaped box on the chair, at the flanged arrangement over the hole, feeling his erection throb away as he did so. He picked the instrument up with both hands, reverently, and sat down.

Looking out over the twilit zone atmosphere, gently plinking the instrument, the idea of what he felt he had to do suddenly dawned on him. I got to get away   got to get away

135

from all the bitches, the dope, this terrible fast life I'm leading, the music I'm playing "The Concerto for Bassssooon, Kanooooon!" echoed in his ear. The Concerto, shit! that's been done already, time to move on.

Why should that fuck with me? he'd asked himself many times, everybody wants to hear what a dude got made on. Duke Ellington still has to play "Sophisticated Lady" every now 'n then to keep 'em cooled out. If Dolphy had lived, he might be getting requests for "Aggression."

He wandered up and down the keyboard, settling on certain patterns and then reversing them, a soulful, melodic refrain happening, playing on for the very first time, an instrument that he had only been playing at.

Yeahhhh ... got to get away, his spontaneously composed tune said to him. Got to get off into another music, yeahhhh, another music. The thought of it, coming to him so simply and directly, jammed both of his thumbs down on the metal flanges and held them there.

A Jazz Quartet for Thumb Piano.

He looked down at the box in his hands and felt tears spring to his eyes because he didn't know the African name for it.

Africa ... yeahhhh, Africa ... that would be a good, good place to go and get my shit together, the Quartet together. Yeahhhh, Africa. He stood, kissed the wooden box solemnly and replaced it on the chair and gracefully jumped from the low stage.

Yeahhhh suhhh, Africa that's sho' 'nuff where I need to go, Momma Africa.

Bessie Mae Black fluttered her eyes open, stifled a yawn remembering her duty and shook Fred Lee's shoulders gently. "Fred! Fred! you better wake up, baby it's 6:30."

Fred grumbled something vaguely obscene and buried his head deeper in the pillow.

136

Bessie looked lovingly at the back of his head, wishing that their roles were reversed, that she was the one who had to hit it on this cold Tuesday morning. "Fredddd," she murmured in his ear

"Yeahhhh, I heard you, it's time to get up," he said loudly in clear, theatrical tones, and turned toward her, to snuggle his face into her big, warm breasts.

She locked her arms around his head, loving him.

"Heyyyy, you better loose me, unless you want me to smother to death . . . or . . . ." He leaned up on his right elbow with a seductive smile on his face.

Bessie met his look with a warm glow in her own eyes, saying, in essence, if you have to go, you have to go, but if you want to stay, that's cool too.

His smile faded, was replaced by a more serious, dedicated look. He knew he had to go to work, that was his responsibility. He kissed her gently on the mouth, eyes and scrambled out of bed, heading for the chair with his pants on it. "That's the way to do it," he said over his shoulder as he hopped to the door, his bare feet chilled by the icy floor. "If you jive around you'll never make it."

He peeked out into the hallway to see if the bathroom was vacant, saw that it was and scurried to take his morning piss.

Bessie huddled down under the covers, vicariously feeling the cold floor, the frozen hallway, the icy bathroom. Who would ever have believed that Fred Lee would be hopping out of bed in deep November, making it to a gig, for love?

She pulled the covers around her shoulders a little more snugly and stared at the slightly open door, wondering did jail change him that much?

It must have, she decided. He wasn't anything like he is now after he came back from Vietnam. After Vietnam they had taken up where they'd left off. Bessie working, Fred Lee chili pimpin' and trying to be nickel slick, promising matri-

137

mony   someday.

What was it Big Momma used to say? "Maybe fightin' them Vietnamese had made him scared o' work."

Bessie shook her head at the echo of Big Momma's words in her head. No, Vietnam hadn't made him lazy. He had told her many times in different ways exactly what being in Vietnam, fighting yellow men for the white man, had done to him.

And then the bust, at Slick Rina and Taco's crib, almost five years ago, five years of waste.

And now the post jail period. What had they done to him in the joint?

He had come out walking tall, talking to her about the new lifestyle he wanted to design for them, the first section of that being that she wouldn't be working any more. He would, he told her, even if it meant shoveling shit with a teaspoon.

Bessie sighhhed, her nose just over the cover's edge, listening to him pad back through the hall. It was rough, being an ex-con but, because of his honorable discharge, he had been able to find a job as a mail clerk in a big department store out in the suburbs, one of those places that didn't have a rehabilitated Negro on the premises and needed one or three badly. In walks bruh Lee.

At any rate, she uncovered her mouth as he popped back in, chill bumps on his arms, she hadn't had to hit a lick at a snake since he got out. "Baby, you want me to get up 'n fix you some breakfast?"

"Nawww, I'll have some coffee 'n a doughnut soon as I get to work," he answered, moving energetically around the room to brush his teeth, wash his face, neck and underarms and to add socks, shoes and turtleneck sweater to his pants.

She wanted to ask him, "Baby, ain't you cold?" but knew it would sound silly, so she simply lay in place, watching him comb out his Afro   gettin' ready to go meet the Man.

Yeahhhh   what the hell *had* happened in the joint?

138

She stared at his lean hips, the bold, definite way he did things. Funny, she thought, it used to be that they would ship brothers off to prison and they'd return like whipped dogs, tails dragging between their legs. But not any more, not if Fred Lee was any example; "I don't want my beautiful black queen to be off slavin' under some blue-eyed devil, it's bad enough that one of us is forced to do it," was one of the first beautiful things he'd said, and then followed that with other, equally beautiful statements and actions. "They be tryin' to practice genocide on us and we be helpin' 'em. Well, that shit must cease. We needs all the lil' beautiful black sons 'n daughters we can get."

Of all things! Fred Lee wanted a baby

She slid her hand down across her stomach   with no pills, no coil, no diaphragm, no condoms, no what did they call it? coitus interruption. It shouldn't be too much longer now, not the way they were keepin' each other awake at night.

And, "Now here's my plan, Bess baby   all we have to do for a year is keep expenses to a bare ass minumum, don't piss off any   well, not too much dough, save every stinkin' cent I make and rent a damed storefront, open up a day nursery or somethin', you dig? Get off into somethin' of our very own."

"Fred, don't you want some toast or somethin' before you go out in the cold?"

He strode over to the side of the bed, his cap at a rakish angle, his topcoat buttoned, pulling on his gloves, his eyes sweeping from her hips to her face and back. "What I want, right now, would be somethin' hotter than any piece o' toast anybody ever had."

She brushed the covers down from her shoulders, ignoring the cold, and reached her arms out to him.

He sprawled across her body and kissed her, deeply.

"Hey, I'll be runnin' late in a lil' bit," he whispered, pushing himself up reluctantly.

She released her hold around his shoulders just as reluctantly, whispering back, a tremor in her voice. "I'll have a nice hot supper for you when you get in tonight."

"You better have!" he said gruffly, humorously, patted her on the ass and split.

She sprawled herself out, goose pimpled arms played out beside her, aroused, in love, feeling for her man clattering down the stairs to catch a cold bus in the cold dawn for a trip to the cold, white suburbs.

"Fred?" she had asked him one night, having gone to the laundromat, grocery shopped, cleaned the apartment twice, and done a dozen other little things to make their life groovier. "Fred, they don't hardly have any black people goin' out as far as you do, do they?"

He had almost swallowed a fish bone laughing at her. "Oh wowwww! Baby you talk, you talk like one o' them civil wahh niggers!"

"Well, you can call me whatchu will or may, all I know is how ugly some of those white dudes can be, 'specially the middle-aged ones   way out there."

"Bessie," he had fixed her with a hard look, "I been through enough shit in my young life to get me ready for anything. Are you hip to the fact that I did time in *'Nam and the joint?* And I still ain't but twenny-seven. I wish one o' them silly motherfuckers would even look at me wrong!"

She stared at the clock on the bedside stand. 7:05. He was on the bus now, probably napping to the first transfer point. She stuffed her arms back under the cover, wishing she could dream some money into being as she settled in for another hour's sleep before her guilt complex forced her to get up, to do something, anything.

Think I'll talk to him about workin' again, this evenin', at least until I get pregnant, she told herself and drifted back

140

off   mocking the cold sunshine of another day that was telling practically everybody else in the neighborhood to get up, get out and scuffle again.

Requiem for Mr. Chickens

The people of the community, honest johns, jiffy slicksters, peanut pushers, one-stop do-droppers, duece 'n' dice guys, three-card molly players, innocents of all ages, children, mushmouth sisters, down home gossipers, snuff dippers, exotic religionists, fast steppers, high rollers and just plain ol' folks, walked past the Spinning Top Dude, the wind shoveling cold air up their cracks, glancing, if they paid any attention to him at all, at his slow work with a beautiful hourglass top made of Swedish crystal, as he spooled it up and down a spider's web string, singing sadly in his native Tagalog all the while.

They may have smiled discreetly or laughed quickly, openly, at the sight of his friend Mr. Chickens sprawled out on a pile of cold, crusted garbage, nose snuggled down in a bag of chicken bones ironically, either asleep or dead drunk.

"Hey, did y'all hear about Mr. Chickens!?"

Nathan Holt looked up glumly from his Tuesday evening newspaper, his slippered feet propped up on a box of packed chinaware.

"Yes, Byron, I heard about it. Wasn't that a shame? They say the poor man laid out there all day before anybody came to get him," Diane Holt answered, bustling around, packing.

"What did he die from?" Nathan asked, a cynical curl to his lips.

"They say he froze to death," Byron answered sadly.

"Why didn't his buddy, what do you all call him?"

"The Spinnin' Top Dude."

"Yeah, why didn't he help him?"

141

Byron shrugged, "People say he was too drunk."

Nathan grumbled, flexed his newspaper out and stuck his face back into the sports page.

"Well, all I can say is, it's a shame that people would let a person lay up in a pile o' garbage all day and not try to give him some kind of help. Byron, come on back here 'n help me get some o' this stuff off the shelf in the back closet. Lawd ha' mercy, I didn't know we had so much junk. Nathan, don't press your heels down on that box 'n break my dishes." Mother Holt scurried through the short hallway leading to the rear of the apartment, her youngest son plodding along obediently behind her.

Nathan scowled in the direction of their exit, looked around at the shadowed places where pictures had been removed, at the boxes of mysteriously wrapped up bits of family history, piled up odds and ends of a ten-year occupancy, and scowled again. Moving   shit! Buyin' a damned house. What if I lost my job? The way things is these days, ain't no tellin' what's gon' happen.

He lowered his newspaper onto his lap, leaned his head back onto the headrest of the chair and dozed off, thinking negative thoughts, a secure island in the middle of a sea of packed household goods, ready for relocation.

Perry opened the door quietly, peeked around at his father and motioned for his true blue ladyfriend to come in.

Nathan opened his eyes slowly, felt for a second that he was looking at a very young version of Pearl Bailey.

"Hi, Mr. Holt, did we wake you up?"

"Oo, ahhemmm, naw! I was just   uhhh   checkin' my eyelids for holes, come on in. I would ask you to sit down but, as you can see, Diane got the whole place boxed up."

"Where is Momma, Daddy?"

Diane sang out over the distance, "I'm back here, whose voice is that I hear?"

142

"It's Rochelle's, Momma!" Perry called back, a smile in his voice.

"Rochelle?! Rochelle, come on back here, honey . . . I got some baby pictures of Perry and Byron to show you."

Father and son surreptitiously checked out Rochelle's well-designed figure from the rear, as she darted away gleefully to see photos of her roommate to be.

"They sho' as hell wasn't makin' 'em like that when I was comin' 'long," Daddy Holt obliquely congratulated his son on his choice, impressed once again.

Perry slapped his father's outstretched left hand lightly, affirmatively.

They exchanged brief, soulful looks.

"Looks about like everything is ready to go, huh?"

"Yep, just about   but you know your mother, she keeps findin' somethin' else that needs to be boxed up."

Perry smiled at his old man's mock weary complaint and the cackling noises coming from the women, coupled to the heavier sound of Byron's polite laughter.

"Byron back there?"

"Yeah, he's helpin' pack." Nathan dug into his shirt pocket for his cigarettes, offered Perry one.

"Nawww, not me. I'm gon' be dyin' from too many other things as it is."

"Right on, son! Right on! If I had just turned twenny-two, I wouldn't be suckin' on these ol' coffin nails myself, but I ain't got a thing to lose, not at my age   coff off!"

Perry leaned his weight from foot to foot, feeling strangely awkward. "Daddy?"

"Huh?"

"I   uhhh

The two men exchanged evasive expressions for a few seconds.

"Go 'head, boy . . . spit it out, you know you can say any-

143

thing you got a mind to, to me."

"Uhhh,   well . . . ."

A fresh series of cackles and tenor chuckles cut him off.

"Ain't like you to be tie-tongued, Perry," his father teased him, blowing smoke rings.

Perry took the bait. "Well, what I wanted to say to you was   uhhh, I won't be makin' this move with the family."

Nathan Holt's shoulders shook as he coughed and laughed. "Shit! I thought you was gon' tell me somethin' spectacular. You ain't been doin' nothin' but talkin' about gettin' married for the last six months. Naturally we took it for granted that you'd either do one or two things   either you 'n Rochelle live with us 'til y'all found a place of your own that you like or just live with us period, there's room a'plenty in that big ol' hairy place."

Perry chewed on his bottom lip. "That's a beautiful idea, Daddy   it sho' 'nuff is, but

"No buts! We'll be puttin' all this junk on a truck Saturday mornin', hightailin' it to the land of saddidy niggers."

Perry flashed a large grin in his father's direction, in appreciation of the joke, and looked down at his shoes.

"Well? what's the matter? Ain't this what everybody in the family wanted?"

"Momma did anyway   hahhhahhhah," Perry replied, knowing exactly what had gone down between his mother and father on the house deal.

Nathan released a long smile and waited, feeling vaguely uneasy with his favorite son's ambivalence about, about? What the hell was it about?

They were suddenly silent, the chatter from beyond filling up the dead space.

"Daddy, me and Rochelle have decided to live   to set up housekeepin' together," Perry blurted out.

Nathan Holt's first impulse reaction was to ask, "And not

get married at all?" But he cooled it out and said instead, "Is that a fact?"

"Yeah!" Perry rushed on, bending over to place his palms on his knees in his excitement. "See, the way we've figured it out, with my stuff packed 'n everything, what sense would it make to be movin' all of my stuff out to the house? When all I'd be doin' is movin' it a lil' later on anyway."

Father Holt sucked hard on the back end of his coffin nail, inwardly disappointed at the idea of not having his favorite son with him awhile longer. "Shack job, huh?" he asked, not really intending to be as crude as the question sounded.

Perry unintentionally made a perfect imitation of his father's scowl. "Well, if you wanna call it that, the thing is, Daddy Rochelle has an apartment, she's workin', I'm workin' 'n goin' to school 'n everything, so I mean, like, in a way, we felt it would be easier to get off into our own thang just that much sooner."

Nathan looked around for an ashtray, couldn't find one, stubbed his cigarette out on a crate marked "water glasses." And lit up immediately thereafter. He took a few drags, getting himself together before saying anything. "What do her folks think?"

"Oh, it's cool with them."

He took a couple more drags. "You told your Momma about this?"

Perry shook his head, negative-negative.

Nathan nodded his head a few times, picturing the scene that would go down, knowing something of his wife's conservative ways. Perry, also in on the know, opened his mouth, prepared to give an oration in favor of shackin', if necessary, but found himself cut off by the sound of approaching feet.

"Perry!" his mother burst into the room. "Rochelle tells me that you all are plannin' to live together 'til March and then get married, sort of a trial marriage, is that right?"

145

Perry nodded up and down primly, feeling almost timid.

Diane Holt circled her prospective daughter-in-law's waist protectively and announced in her sternest voice. "Awright now, I don't want no jive outta you! Come March I want to be standin' up in church watchin' my oldest son and his beautiful woman tie the knot."

The three men exchanged looks in fugal fashion. Momma? Momma!? Diane!!?

"Nathan!" Mrs. Holt continued, adding one amazement to the next, "why don't you put on your shoes 'n run down to the liquor store and get us a lil' somethin'? I've got some homemade egg nog in the box."

Byron strolled over to shake his brother's hand for no particular reason, as Father Holt slowly aroused himself, like someone being shaken from a deep dream.

Diane surreptitiously winked to Rochelle and pulled her back through the hallway to unleash more women's wiles on her receptive young brain.

"Keep 'em stumblin' over each other, honey," she mumbled out of the corner of her mouth, con style, "and make 'em think they've got everything understood before you whip your truth on 'em. The more you do that, the less able they'll be to figurin' you out   then, they'll begin to respect you as a mature woman."

Rochelle nodded coolly, understanding it all, and turned to smile at the picture framed through the hallway of the three men looking slightly bewildered.

Ed and Charlotte Franklin snuggled down under their electric blanket, smoking a last, before-we-go-off-to-sleep cigarette. The cigarette tips glowed in the chilled darkness as they discussed all of the matters that happened to run across their minds. Tuesday spinning out.

"Now you know somebody must've known the po' man was

146

dead, layin' up on a pile o' garbage like that all day."

"Who could tell? Hell, I've seen 'im sprawled out in the alley a dozen times."

Their conversation was interrupted by the muffled sounds of Lubertha coming in, trying not to disturb her parents. They both listened intently, sensitive to any sound that might indicate problems. From their bedroom, following her movements, they could tell that she was o.k., walking heavily, a little more tired that unual, that she had gotten a piece of cold chicken from the 'fridge and a glass of milk or maybe a brew, and that she was off to bed. Neither one spoke for a minute, and then both at once.

"Did she?"—"You know?"

"Go 'head, what were you gon' say?" Ed Franklin conceded.

"I was just goin' to ask you if she had told you about what happened with her Club thing?"

"Yeahhh," he answered and took a deep breath, "really hurt 'er too. We had a lil' talk about it the other night   She called it a perfect case of 'in-ternal dissension.' "

"I call it plain ol' arguin' 'n squabblin'."

"Yeahhh, that's about what it was too."

"So what's happenin' now? From what I can see all she does is mope around with a long face."

"Well, from what she tells me," Ed Franklin started in, swelling with pride at the fact that he and his daughter communicated, "she plans to just stick with her writin', doin' her own thang for the people as she puts it."

"That's really too bad she had to drop out of that thing, 'specially since her and Kweino   "

"Kwendi," he corrected her abruptly.

"Kwendi   Lawwwd, will I ever get that boy's name right? Anyway it's really too bad, after all the time 'n effort and everything else they've been through because of that

147

thing."

"I don't think it's too bad," Ed responded, viciously crushing his cigarette out in the bedside ashtray. "She was too damned good for 'em in the first place."

Charlotte smiled in the darkness, rolled over on her side, lapped her arm across her man's chest and gave him a light squeeze. "You're really proud of her, ain't you?"

"Damned right I am, you don't find daughters like Lubertha growin' on trees."

"Too bad we didn't have that boy you wanted, to go 'long with her."

He kissed the bridge of her nose tenderly, "We can make another stab at it if you want to?"

She moved away slightly, digging him in the ribs. "Ed, behave yourself!" she cautioned him humorously. "If I came up pregnant now, at my age, they'd have to take both of us to the hospital."

They shared a quiet little sniggle-giggle session and settled down on their respective sides of the bed, glad that the week was at its midway point and that Lubertha was their daughter.

148

Chapter 7

Making the Sheets Work

Chili tried to ignore the sunlight streaming in on him, the brightness making his eyelids flutter. He changed his position in bed, hoping to evade it in that way but had no luck

11:48 a.m., Wednesday goddamnit!

Finally pissed off at not being able to evade the gleaming rays, he popped out of bed muttering, "Goddamnit! It's 'sposed to be wintertime, why in the fuck don't it snow some more, or rain or somethin'?" and closed the blinds.

He stood at the window with the drawstring in one hand, scratching his crotch with the other hand, feeling disgusted, fuzzy headed, dopey. He looked back at the rumpled bed and realized that he was up, finally.

Oh well, what the hell, guess I had to get up sometime.

He pulled his bathrobe on, yawning, and shuffled through

the front room, blinking past the wide slit in the drapes, into the kitchen, his mind slowly beginning to function again. Making coffee and toast, he began to think seriously about the scene he had been a part of the night before

Running into Jake the Fake down in the 'hood, smoking good 'erb at Taco and Rina's place with Leo Terry and Harry Mathews ... Jake the Fake taking them all off into this grand scheme he had. Could it work? Chili asked himself as he wandered into the front room, drinking his second cup.

Yeahhh, I wonder, could it work?

He stood in the wide slit of the drapes, the sun a little less menacing now, delicately sipping his coffee and raking Jake the Fake's game back and forth in his mind. The more he thought about it, the more enthusiastic he became, especially about certain sections of the scheme.

He ladled it out again, reviewing the major points Jake had made. "Awright y'all, here it is, listen close 'cause I may not be able to say this as well the second time around."

Chili, a regular from way back when, was allowed the privilege of hearing the scheme with an option to be in. He had listened very closely.

The premises behind the scheme were simple. Most white folks think they're crazy, or that niggers are; so what Jake proposed to do   using Taco and Rina as supersisters and Leo and Harry as superbrothers, was to start an encounter group. Chili had almost laughed at the suggestion, at first ... 'til Jake got really heavy into it.

"Now dig it, we've all done enough time, or been involved in enough 'git yo' soul!' rap sessions to know how to carry off a group therapy thing, right? Awright, so that's what we be doin', for awhile. The most important thing ... I repeat, sisters 'n brothers, the most important thing about this whole project is the proposal that has to be written.

"What we do is this; we go to the nearest anti-poverty

150

office, and I'm certain everybody here knows where that is, the place placed in our community to make sure we all remain po'. What we do, let's say   uhh, Taco and Harry go in as concerned members of the community, use hook 'n crook to get to the white boy in charge."

"How you know it's gon' be a white boy, Jake?" Leo had asked. "They got a lotta brothers sittin' in them high priced chairs these days."

"If the motherfucker is black as my momma's telephone, he's still gon' be white. You know goddamned well whitey wouldn't dare trust an authentic nigger with no white power, meaning money   no sirreee. At any rate, after these two ignunt actin', crazy behavin' motherfuckers have laid the groundwork, me and Leo follow them up with briefcases in hand, talkin' supersuave shit out of both corners of our mouths   assurin' this dude that we have a solution for what ails him.

"Now dig it! Put your hand down, Rina! You ain't in no classroom. Dig it! One of the things we definitely know is this, any kind of proposition you can come up with, to reassure the white boy that you know how to cool niggers out, will get you a hearin'   what did you wanna say, Rina?"

"I just wanted to ask why it had to be Taco 'n Harry . . .?"

"Don't make no fuckin' difference, any of us could go in and mau-mau the fuck outta the dude   The important thing is that he be convinced that the situation can only be handled by people like ourselves. We can even make our sheets work for us, you know, use your record as a resume sort of."

"Hey Jake?" Leo had leaned on him, frowning. "You wouldn't be tryin' to run a game on us, would you?"

"Looka'here, brother, I got bigger, fatter and better chickens to pluck. Don't insult me like that. Any other questions, pertinent ones, that is?"

"Yeahhh," Chili had asked, intrigued by the implications

151

of the proposed play on the white psyche. "How you gonna convince this pootbutt that havin' a group thang would be beneficial to anybody?"

"Good question. The answer is, it's gonna be interracial, which means that it'll offer a few token liberal white broads a chance to give up a lil' stank, in addition to offerin' their sons, husbands, boyfriends, fathers, or whoever, a chance to git shat on, which is what a whole lot of 'em dig. They haven't been havin' too much good nigger shit thrown in their faces since the '60s. But see, look, all of this shit is besides the point 'cause what we need to get it all the way off the ground is   a proposal.

"The proposal is like, it's like, well, you know how it is whenever some important white boy gets assassinated, they appoint a committee to investigate it, right? Right! Awright, the same kind of scene operates in another way   If you wanna get some anti-poverty money in this country, or damned near anything else from the government, you have to come up with a Pro-posal.

"Now *we* know and *they* probably do too, that there ain't a circle in the world that's ever gonna solve any of our racial problems, but that's besides the point, the government likes to help people bullshit themselves, it keeps the heat off the White House. All they have to do is point the finger and say 'See, see what we did, we gave them niggers down there in the ghitto fifty g's to git they shit straight and lookit at what happened?' But in order to shake some of that mad money loose, we need a proposal."

"I can get that proposal together," Chili recalled himself saying, and almost regretted it the second the words popped out of his mouth. Almost. Like, what if . . .?

He looked up from his coffee cup into her merciless blue eyes, staring at him from across the street, and then down to the pink nipples and finally, down to a lush growth of blond

152

bush.

Well, well, I'll be goddamned!

Playing his role to the bus-stop, he squatted and sat his cup and saucer on the floor, stood up slowly, untied his robe, placed his hands on his hips underneath the robe and swayed back and forth, dangling an invitation.

The two figures studied each other for a few long minutes, an existentialistic dilemma hanging them both up.

She moved back from the window and lasciviously crooked her forefinger at him, "Come," it said, "come and play games."

Chili, equal to the moment, backed up a few steps himself, dropped his robe from his shoulders, sensually gripped his semi-erect penis with his right hand and beckoned with its head   "You come, over here," it said, and then he quickly closed the drapes.

He hurried over to the record player, reloaded the spindle with Miles' "New Directions," rushed to the toilet to brush his teeth and comb his hair.

Nawwww, fuck it! he decided when he got to his Afro, that's what the bitch is on her way over here for, to dig her fingers into my nappy ass hair.

Teeth brushed, a lil' cologne slapped on his jaws, he coolly unlocked the front door and returned to his bedroom to smoke a joint while he waited for the freak bitch from across the street.

Which one was it? He tried to place her. Which one was it? He had seen about five altogether, but she didn't seem to be one of them   New blood then, what the fuck!

Could Jake's scheme work? Yeah, yeah it could work if Cynthia wrote the kind of proposal they needed, an airtight, fantastic piece of bureaucratic bullshit   mau-maued into place by the right kind of militant niggerism. Say a hundred grand split six ways. Cynthia?

153

Nawwww, what the hell would she do with more money?

Two-hundred grand   that'd be more like it. The more you ask for, the more you get. Yeahhhh, it would work, but all of us would have to be triple quick 'n slick on our jobs.

His heart thumped a couple odd times as the tall blond girl appeared in the doorway of the bedroom. "You lock the door behind you?" he asked coldly, masking his nerves.

She nodded yes and asked with a sly smile, in a deep Southern drawl, "What's your name?"

"Did you come over here to interview me or gimme some pussy?"

She blinked uncontrollably a few times and broke into a long toothed, Fly Me, Glistereen toothpaste smile. "Dorothy and Susanne and Barbara and,   ohh, ahl the gurls have been tellin' me how crazy you were, lak, how you leave the blinds of your bedroom winder open 'n stuff."

Chili gazed evenly into her face. Big ol' lush cornfed blond bitch, magnolia blossoms dripping from her jibs. "Yeah, I be doin' shit like that 'cause I be tryin' to thrill the whole neighborhood. Come over here, I know you get high, don't you?" He shoved the half-smoked joint out to her.

"Nawwww," she drawled softly, digging down into her coat pocket, "I don't rally care too much for grass, I kinda lak coke a lil' bit more. You?"

Chili moved with a supercasual air to flick the fire at the end of the joint out in his swan-shaped ashtray. Welllll, welllll, welll . . . look what the wind just blew in, from right across the street too.

He nodded yes, yes, I dig coke and scooched himself up in bed, nostrils flared for the cocaine's reception. "Yeah, I dig coke. Here, put a lil' bit right here before we snort." He cupped his member up between his hands at her.

The blonde smiled lazily, stepped out of her shoes, pulled a vial of cocaine out of her pocket and slid her coat off of

154

her naked shoulders.

Chili's penis twitched and throbbed, receiving the stimuli.

"You musta damned near froze walkin' over here," he observed.

"No, no way, not hot as ah'm feelin'," she replied, already loaded, and bent over to smear the alkaloid crystals around the ridges of his penis, carefully wedging a few grains into the tip and opening.

Chili watched the whole operation with cold, analytical eyes. Wowww, this bitch is really on her job. Yeahhh, Jake's thing would work, a really hip nigger could practically get white folks to do anything, if he was willing to act crazy enough.

I have to put Cynthia's educated ass on that proposal tomorrow. Yeahhh, a couple hundred grand would sho' 'nuff be a nice sting. He stared, fascinated at the sight of the naked woman sitting on the side of the bed snorting from a tiny spoon.

"Why haven't your girlfriends taken up my invite? I've been holdin' it out to 'em for a lil' while now."

"Maybe they don't know how good dark meat rally is," she replied and passed the spoon under his left nostril.

The Honorable Reverend Father Love stretched himself on the long, low, plush sofa in his dressing room, crossing his legs from time to time as Marvin Weinstock, his accountant, agent, lay attorney, valet, boon cool companion and hip aide-de-camp doused his mind with figures, twenty minutes before his Wednesday evening telecast. "So, there it is, Daddy," Marvin concluded. "You're way ahead of the game, you could split the scene tomorrow and live happily ever after, wherever."

"Marvin!" Father Love chastized him in a friendly-furious fashion, "I'll thank you to leave off with that 'Daddy' shit, and those absurd remarks you're always makin' about me splittin'. How could I leave all of my loyal followers in such a bind?"

"And all that gravy you'd be missing."

"Right on! And all that unsopped up gravy."

The two men exchanged warm, confidential smiles.

"Oh yeah, Dad   uhh   Reverend Love, I forgot to tell you, we've lined up a really great Swahili teacher for you."

"Beautiful! beautiful! That's wonderful. I was beginning to get worried. I couldn't imagine anything worse than an East African tour not knowing how to rap. How long do you think it'll take me to learn the language?"

"For anybody else, I'd say six months, for you   three."

Once again they exchanged their special set of smiles.

A rapid clack of knocks on the door froze them both into more serious expressions.

"Yes!" Father Love boomed out.

"Ten minutes, sir!" a harried, metallic voice squeaked from the other side of the door.

"Thank you, Bobby!" Father Love called back and turned to Marvin. "You'll have to leave me now, Marv   I must meditate at this time, get my thoughts together."

Marvin Weinstock stood, clutching a sheaf of financial statements, and smirked knowingly   Meditation shit! Cocaine or maybe a dexi was more like it. "O.k., Father, I'll see you after the show. Don't forget about those people we have to talk to tonight about the southern tour." The self proclaimed Honorable Reverend Father Love waved him out of the door with a gracious gesture and folded his hands on his ample belly, eyes closed.

God! life sho' is sweet.

He nodded for a few quick moments, unable to forget the tiresome Sunday afternoons of being forced to visit widows and talk shit, to fuck 'em whenever it became necessary, evade

156

hip, militant young motherfuckers who were always trying to mess his thang up, git on! Yeahhh, life sho' was sweet.

He clenched his eyelids tightly, trying to remember the last time he had had an authentically good time. What is it the old ladies used to say God don't love ugly? Sister Sadie was a good feeling. Just feeling her titties could make you come and fuckin' her was like melting into a bowl of fat meat, but she was always good for a tenspot or a twenny if she had gotten her check or if Baby June hadn't beaten her out of it.

"Five minutes to go, Father Love, will you please come and take your place, sir?"

Father Love looked at the small girlish figure leaning around the corner of the doorway and smiled roguishly.

White folks love money so much they'll even kiss a nigger's ass if he gets enough of it   Look at this punk ass

"Son, you may not know it but I'm in my place right now."

The "gopher" shook his head, puzzled, unaccustomed to the ways of sharp black prophets.

Father Love, enjoying the bewildered expression on the young man's pale face, held a hand crusted with jewels out to him. "Gimme a hand here, young stuff . . . you may not know where I'm comin' from, but I sho' in hell do."

Bobby rushed over to the side of the sofa and helped Father Love sit up, feeling, as usual, under his spell.

"We have to hurry, sir   The director likes to have everyone in place well before t.v.t., as   you   uhh know."

"Fuck Arthur J. Bowers in his left nut! He can't have no television time unless I'm here. I am the Honorable Reverend Father Love, the First, and none of this shit would be happenin' if it wasn't for me. Can you dig where I'm comin' from, young stuff?"

Bobby the Gopher reddened slightly and helped the good Father drape a Liberace-lame cape over his shoulders.

"Now then, let's git it on," he said, and placed his left hand

157

on Bobby's right shoulder, to be led, as though he were some sort of potentate, onto the set.

Bobby almost enjoyed the job of leading Father Love to his place on the set, that is, when there weren't any strangers around, people who didn't understand. One day his parents had come to a taping of the show and, his Dad especially, had gotten highly pissed, seeing Father Love's arrogance at work on their only son.

Father Love swept his cape back from his left shoulder, Vincent Price playing Cyrano de Bergerac. "Lead on, young blood," Father cooed to Robert Hirshfeld, would-be television producer. "Lead on, lead me back in front of that pot o' gold again tonight."

Bobby walked slowly, anxiety crinkling his brow, Father Love's hand surprisingly heavy on his shoulder, through the corridor leading to the set, trying to figure out how one could gain control of a black shyster prophet-preacher who was netting something like a mil a year. Maybe I should talk to Marvin, get the ins 'n outs of it.

Father Love pinched his shoulder, "Think ye not evil thoughts, young stuff for it has been written that only the Lawd giveth and only the Lawd have the power to taketh it away."

"Amen!" Bobby seconded his sarcasm with a taste of his own and led him to his aluminum coated throne, a sparkling feast on television.

"Places everybody!" the producer yelled, followed by the director screaming the same thing.

Father Love slowly fixed his face into the expression he wanted it to be when he channeled into ten-million lonely, religious women and confused, blundering men.

Yessss, Lawd a'mighty, life sho' is sweet . . . he mumbled to himself as he watched the announcer begin his buildup-intro. Yessss, Lawd a'mighty, life sho' is sweet!!

158

The Great Lawd Buddha buttoned the top button of his rough, heavy woolen pajamas, pulled his blankets up under his chin and laced his hands behind his head, gazing through the barred cell window at the bristling stars beyond. He shivered slightly, not from actual cold, but from the thought of it.

Never could stand the cold too well, always loved the warm more than the cold.

He looked away from the squared-off picture of the bright moon and stars, over to his writing table, a small wooden version of a card table, ignoring the loud, snuffly noises of his cellmate, Ranklin C. Jones, holdup man, dreaming on his bunk against the opposite wall.

Buddha lay, wide awake, filtering the hundreds of midnight jail sounds   the snoring, whispered escape plans, blues hummers, coughers, the squealings of homosexual assaults, the groan and grunt of homosexual relations, the dazzling array of mad sounds that could only come from caged men.

He sat up on the side of his bunk, feeling restless, feeling the urge to write.

Wonder what kind of bullshit Daddy Love laid on the spellbound American public this evening?   Oh well, guess I'll have to wait for the grapevine edition at breakfast.

He smiled at the thought as he pulled the table across the narrow distance to his knees, draped his blankets over his shoulders, across his knees and sat, alternately staring through the window and down at the notebook and pencils on the table in front of him.

He finally opened the notebook, frowned at the smudge marks on the first five pages, a legacy of Ranklin C. Jones' surreptitious interest, and read up to where he had stopped writing the night before. "I think the geography book is what carried me off into fantasia, in the Beginning."

He picked up one of the pencils beside the notebook, checked the point in the bright glare of the moonshine and began to write, the moon and stars seeming to offer more light with the formation of each word. "How could I *not* be carried off, in the Beginning, down there in that racial swamp?"

He stirred his pencil around in midair for a few seconds, mentally reviewing the six lynchings he had watched from a distance in his boyhood, and the far more numerous ones he had managed to escape from actin' uppidy in Mississippi, America.

"Yeah, it was the geography book that carried me off," he continued, "reading about far away places and other kinds of people. Anything would have done it," he thought as he wrote, "anything at all, a soft word, a gentle look, electric lights, an indoor toilet, maybe the hooting of a midnight flyer, but it was none of those, it was the geography book."

Settling into stride, he crossed his ankles and pulled the blankets tighter around his shoulders.

"God only knows how I came across the damned thing. If my memory serves me correctly, we only had twelve books in our whole big one room schoolhouse, and none of them had a range of thought beyond "Lil' Black Sambo," the "Family in the Cotton Fields" and such like, but one day, as such things do happen   there it was   tattered, battered and readable, with pictures yet.

"I can recall even now, oh so clearly, how pissed off I was to come to the African section of the book and find all the people, looking so black and strange. But that was years ago, thank God! And I've since developed a more sophisticated view of blackness."

He paused, smiling, as he watched Ranklin C. Jones moan and sensually rub his testicles.

"Everything was strange in that book, the people, the words (it took quite awhile to understand those), the statistics, the names, all of it! That is, 'til I began to make my own framework for all of it.

"I find myself constantly referring to something that I call the Beginning. For want of a better word, I guess I'll have to stay there, for a few emotional beats, before I go on to the upper levels of purgatory. The strong, always tired, black, dirt-working robots who happened to be my parents and all of the relatives who looked and acted pretty much the way they did, were not the Beginning, nor was that clapboard shack with the old newspapers wadded into the cracks, nor was the white man who had the power of life and death over us, mostly death.

"No, it was the odor of places I'd never smelled, the look in a pair of eyes I'd never seen, the urge to wander around inside my soul   that was the Beginning.

"Once released from my external bondage by the power of the book, I wandered around the world, doing the undo-able; I slept with white women, blondes with skins so pale that they had to be pimped before you could believe that they were real, in defiance of all of Mississippi's rules. I climbed Fujiyama, looked the sacred leopard on top of Kilimanjaro in the eye, I ran with the bulls in Pamplona, went off into fern coated shacks with Polynesian goddesses who nursed me through tropical fevers, killed lions and elephants for the favor of the hand of the Oba's daughter. I emigrated to old China on a dilapidated freighter and found myself on the Southside of Chicago, in the middle of the ol' wintertime.

"But what did it matter where I was whenever I closed the book? What did it matter? After I had found that the only thing I had to do was open up a dozen, a hundred, a thou-sand other books that would sweep me away just as quickly."

A heavy bank of clouds oozed across the moon's face, temp-orarily darkening his effort. He waited impatiently for it to pass, aware once again of the richness of night noises in the joint.

161

Somebody typing on the tier below, . . . must be Kwendi. Yeahhh, that would be him, young stud never sleeps it seems, but who am I to talk?

The clouds passed, leaving him temporarily blinded by the re-emergence of the moonlight.

"Leaving Mississippi three steps ahead of the lynch mob and working, bumming, conning, doing whatever else necessary to make life happen was a great book. I wish I had the nerve to try and remember all of it. Starving almost to death in a hermit's shack down in Cairo, Illinois. Why Cairo, Illinois? my imagination said to me. Why not Cairo, Egypt? And I was off   the one room shack became a fifty room hash den owned by a funky-butt Ptolemaic aristocrat.

"It's a very strange thing to admit to yourself, after so long, that you are a liar. But I wonder about me, specifically me, on this score. Have I been a liar all these years, or a geography teacher?"

He frowned at the sound of the toilet being flushed in the cell next to him.

"What does it really matter? After all is said and done about what you are, someone once said, it's what you have done with what you are. And what was I before I was tamed? Before I had the iron doors slammed behind me and the key thrown away?"

The moon glared at the fierce smile he turned up to it.

"What was I? A question that not many men less wise than myself would even attempt to deal with."

He paused, on the verge of writing a lie, before going on with the truth.

"I was a conning, cunning, scheming, dreaming, shrewd, slick, conniving beast, a miniature dinosaur with a brain a lecher, a consummate player. I was, at one time, the Great Lawd Buddha."

He had to stop writing for a moment, to cool out the gush

162

of egotism he felt rising within himself.

"Yes, at one time, I was the Great Lawd Buddha, a super-sonic, geopolitical mac man. There've been times, many times, when I've found myself flashing across the face of the planet, taking those who could come with me, on the strength of a name   Yemen, Jakarta, Hunza, Moeshoeshoe, Lhasa, Huatabampo, Mundina   God! Whatever happened to Mundina? Yes, if not the name of a place, the name of a woman, or her perfume, or the shape of her earlobe.

"I was that, a lover of the lives of the women who thought that the greatest gift they had to offer was their bodies and all I really wanted, in most cases, was their stories."

The sour-sweet memory of Heatwave set off a dull, achy feeling around the region of his heart.

"The ladies of my summer in life, the Circassians, the Navajos, the hundreds of hours of glamorous sorrow I suffered, taking my grizzled lovebone into and out of their holy slits, putting my mind into the position of being given something more precious than all the cunt they could possibly lay on me. Back and forth I've gone, across these United States, this cold-blooded America, from the east to the west, from north to south, tripping into Mexican villages, near Detroit, or raiding the striped tents of rival Bedouins because that's what one did, just this side of the Golden Gate Bridge.

"The moments I've had. The exquisite flavors of ten-thousand make-do stews in a thousand hobo jungles, the glistening stories recited by shattered men with hearts of tempered steel, the little fires, the rivers of wine."

He let the pencil slip out of his fingers and leaned back against the wall, wishing he had a cigarette.

Maybe Rank has one.

He peered across at Ranklin C. Jones, at the smile slicing his brown face in sleep, dreaming of Pam Grier's titties, checked out the area surrounding him and spotted a half-

163

smoked cigar in a jar lid under the edge of his bunk.

Oh well   what the hell

He skirted the edge of his table, stooped for the half-done stogie, found a match and lit up   frowning from the first puff   guess beggars can't be choosy.

He remounted his seat behind the table, the smoke from the cheap cigar, held down too long, giving him a cheap high. He looked closely at the last words he had written, "rivers of wine, rivers of wine, days and nights of frustration, illness, suffering, a lifetime of dismal failure.

"How hard it is to tell the truth. A lifetime of failure. To be able, after all these years, to say that. To say that I've never been to Europe, Africa, Asia, or any other fucking place outside my country 'tis of thee."

He dropped the smouldering cigar butt on the floor, feeling angry. "Making it up as I went along, that's what I did. I made it all up, the windblown feasts on the Mongolian steppes with Kurdish tribesmen,   here's yogurt in your eye!

"The Japanese penis worshipping society, the Great Lawd Buddha, President   down, girls! down!

"The voodoo thang in Papa Doc's Haiti, Erzulie's ride on my back, my career as a nudist photographer on the French Riviera, the kisses I exchanged with the princesses of twelve nations, including that cold-blooded young English bitch who loved horses more than she liked men.

"The rackets, the games, the schemes, the hustles   all lies! Yes, all lies!"

He looked up, surprised to see the sky streaked by the first signs of another day, in this instance, Thursday, but no matter, and hurried on, writing as though the full day would destroy everything he had written.

"My life has been one glorious lie from beginning to end. A lie that deviated from time to time but still remained a lie, or perhaps I should put it another way, where other men have

164

habitually told the truth and lied sometimes, I have always lied and told the truth as seldom as possible   For me a lie . . . ."

"What is it, Buddhaman?" Ranklin yawwwned across at him, ending his story for the moment.

Buddha nodded his head neutrally, plastering his opaque look on.

"You been writin' all night, Buddhaman?"

"That's right, brother, all night long."

Ranklin stepped onto the floor gingerly, popped over to the unenclosed stool for his morning piss. "Mannnnn, I don't see how you do it. I have a helluva time tryin' to scribble my woman a few lines every now 'n then."

Buddha smiled and, along with the rest of the inmates, prepared to deal with another jailhouse day.

"Buddha?" the guard spoke through the bars.

"Yeah, what can I do for you, Smitty?" Buddha turned to him casually, folding his blankets on his bunk, looking forward already to the nap he was preparing to steal later in the day.

"Warden wants to see you."

Buddha straightened up, a shrewd gleam spooling the possible reasons around in his mind. "What's he want, Smitty?"

"Ooohhh, I don't rightly know."

Ranklin winked at Buddha, turned to the guard, working sour against Buddha's sweet. "What the fuck you mean, you don't know! You the motherfuckin' polease here, ain't you?!"

"Mind your own business, Rank. When I got something to say to you, I'll call your name and number, o.k.?"

Ranklin C. Jones, having spent a night dreaming of freedom and ladies, started to bristle up at the guard. Buddha, cool, cooled him out. "It's cool, Rank, it's cool, probably needs my help to figure somethin' out. I'll be ready in a minute, Smitty."

165

Buddha changed into his prison denims, brushed his teeth and shot a natural comb through his receding hairline a few times. "O.k., let's be gettin' on."

Smitty signaled to the gateman to release the current on Buddha's cell, manually unlocked it and glared at Ranklin C. Jones. "Better watch your step, Rank," he warned as he fumbled with his keys.

"Shhhiii-it! if you know what's good for you, you better watch your own fuckin' step   This is our prison, not yours."

Buddha and the guard fell into step on the way to the warden's office, Buddha reviewing his sins of the past week. Wonder what the fuck he wants to see me about? That cocaine deal? Nawww, he wouldn't have any way of knowing about that. The prostitution ring? Nawww, it wouldn't be about that, what the hell do they care about punks setting up a union? The moonshine still in the kitchen? Nawww, not that either, that's been there for years. What?

He maintained a poker face through all the checkpoints, began to feel slightly nervous as they stood in front of the huge paneled door of the warden's office.

Smitty knocked politely, twice.

"Come in!" a big bass voice boomed out.

"The Great   uhhh, Chester Simmons, sir," Smitty announced, ushering him in.

"Come in! Come in! Come in Buddha!   Thank you, Smitty   That'll be all."

The guard reluctantly departed, certain that this man he guarded every day, this passive storyteller, was going to harm his warden in some way.

Buddha stood in the center of the floor, holding his cap behind his back, taking the warden's measure. Big, bluff, bleary-eyed beer drinker, three months in the Chair, tough.

"Sit down, Buddha! Sit down! . . . I know you're wonderin'

166

why I wanted to see you. Coffee?"

"Yes, thank you, sir."

The warden bounced over to his intercom. "Pasquale, two espressos, please."

The Great Lawd Buddha relaxed, placed his cap on his knee espresso, shit! Things couldn't be too bad, not if he was going to be treated to Italian coffee beforehand.

The telephone buzzed twice before the warden snatched it up. Trouble with a couple members of the population.

"Sock both of the bastards in the Hole!" the warden growled, looking at Buddha as though he were a fellow warden, someone who understood the problems of managing the Big House.

Pasquale, the warden's personal servant, knocked lightly and popped in balancing a tray of coffee cups and a pot of coffee like the good Italian-European waiter he had been, once upon a time.

"Pasquale, I don't wanna be disturbed for the next half hour," the warden warned him as he pulled his swiveling armchair around to the front of his desk to sip with Buddha. He handed him a demitasse, poured one for himself and settled his beefy frame into his seat opposite Buddha.

"Now then," he growled jovially, "lemme hear this story about you ruling the city of Tel Aviv for a week without anybody knowing about it. Anybody who can put anything over on them goddamn Jew bastards has got to have a helluva lot on the ball! Hahhhhahhahhahhh!"

The Great Lawd Buddha settled back in his seat, balancing his coffee cup on his thigh, an enigmatic smile on his face. Uhh huhh, so this is what this motherfucker wants, a Scheherazade session, huh? Oh well, espresso is a helluva lot tastier than that chicory dishwater in the mess hall. Guess I better tear that shit up I wrote last night, no one would believe it anyway.

167

He suavely held his cup out for a refill. "Well, Warden, you see, it was like this. I had copped a ride on this ol' freighter, deliverin' coffee from Brazil to Haifa and ...."

Chapter 8

The Proposal

"Awright, there it is, The Proposal," Chili announced after reading the last page of the twenty-five pages Cynthia had devoted all of her liberal energies to, day and night, for a solid month.

Jake the Fake let out a long, low whistle ... "Woww! Bruh Chili, that's a helluva piece o' work you got there, I didn't know you had it in you."

"Uhh, well, I had a lil' help," he replied slyly.

The members of the group looked cautiously at each other, reluctant to give any wholesale endorsement to anything.

"Heyyy mannnn, that's a motherfucker of a proposal, and I ain't just bullshittin' neither," Leo Terry opened up the group.

"Yeah, Chili   it's clean outta sight!"

"Right on!"

Chili flashed the group an arrogant smile and toked up on the joint going around.

"Awright everybody, pull in close and listen up," Jake folded his hands pontifically on Taco and Rina's kitchen table and waited for absolute quiet. "Awright now, we got the proposal. Chili, you got copies for everybody?"

Chili, on his job, reached down into his attache case and pulled out xeroxed copies, passed them around.

"O.k.," Jake continued, "I don't have to tell anybody here that we operatin' in Tricky Dick's land, so beware, be cool, be together."

"Awww com' on, man," Harry growled at him. "We don't need no fuckin' pep talks, git down!"

Jake rolled his eyes malevolently at Harry, cancelled out the urge to say something nasty.

"Uhh huh, o.k. then, here we go. I want it to be understood from the git-go that this is *my* plan but . . . but, if anyone has anything they feel they can add to the basic plan as we go 'long, feel free. What we want is as perfect a thing as we can git together."

He looked deeply into each pair of eyes around the table. "Now then, here is the thang, in steps. Step number one, everybody study that proposal like you've never studied anything in your whole life."

Taco interrupted, staring at her copy of the proposal. "Why you have to have so goddamned many bigass words in this motherfucker?"

" 'Cause that's what the white boy digs," Chili answered smoothly, remembering Cynthia's advice. "Bureaucrats just love to read stuff they find impossible to make any sense of."

"Chili's right," Harry seconded the notion.

"Study the proposal," Jake moved on as though the interruption had never occurred, "know and understand each para-

170

graph of it, especially those money sections. Make damn certain you know and understand all of the reasons why this Mental Energy Encounter Therapy Group, M.E.E.T.G., is necessary. We gon' have classes on it as we go along. The important thing is preparation."

Chili clicked his eyes around at the group, snapping up their rapt expressions. Yeahhh, this shit just might work . . . first time I've ever seen these niggers really into something this deep.

"As well we all know, the proposal was the big, big thang Chili got that for us, the second thing was a location to run the game from. I got that." Jake the Fake held up a real estate lease.

"I got a piece of legal paper that says we've been holdin' Mental Energy Encounter Therapy sessions in this here storefront for the last two years."

"You really cookin', Jake!" Leo exclaimed.

"This paper is strictly legit too. Now then, what we gonna have to do is pull our shit out from under wraps. Our thang is that we been doin' the very best we could on our very own, not askin' anybody for a single bit of help of any kind, doin' maximum good for the community, but now, with times the way they are, we've reached the please-throw-us-a-bone stage."

"With plenny meat on it," Leo added.

"Right on! brother   It'll take a lil' work to set things up, but we can do it if we all pull together with no negative vibes."

"Where we gon' get the right kind o' whiteys for this thing?" Rina asked.

"What do you mean, the right kind?"

"Well," she answered petulantly, "you know, the kind that don't need a lot o' whippin' 'n shit. I ain't about to get off into the business of solvin' no honkie's problems, dig it? I

171

mean, like, this is supposed to be an interracial setup, right?"

"I hear ya, baby   I hear ya," Jake con-smiled at her brightly. "Nawww, dig, we ain't about to become a legit group, under no circumstances. What we'll have, on the white meat side, is a few ol' jive liberal nuns, some o' those do-good protestant ministers, a few unitarian Jews, a few long-hairs, if we can keep 'em from being loaded all the time, three or four 'sensitive' niggers with no prison records and our-selves. Each of us will be like a   a   counselor."

"I just thought I'd lay it out beforehand. I got too much on my own head to be havin' some ol' white broad lay her problems on me too."

"Hey, don't worry 'bout it, Rina baby. We can fake it clean through. Any other questions before we go through our first drill   uhh   rehearsal?"

"Yeah, I got a few," Harry eased in.

"Spill it out, man, 'cause once we go off into this, any doubts, any bad vibes at all will fuck our whole thang up."

"O.k.," Harry began slowly, ticking off points on his fingers. "We got a proposal here that would make me dig down into my pocket for a few coins, if I had any." He paused to lean over to slap Chili's outstretched palm appreciatively. "You got the front we need and we make up the people to pull the sting off. Now then, what I wanna know is this, how can you be so damned certain that we can put this thing into the works and not have it come up a lemon?"

Jake the Fake smiled slightly, his forty years of minor cons having prepared him for such skepticism. He stood and leaned his knuckles on the table. "Brother Mathews, I'm sho' 'nuff glad you asked that there question," he continued, using a Kingfish approach before going on to the serious. "I was gonna save a lil' bit, just in case we had a dropout or two, but seein' as how everybody is deeply involved."

His eyes spun around the group, probing for dropouts,

172

"Since everyone is committed *and* involved with the project, I see no reason to hold back the most vital part of what guarantees the success of this plan."

He paused to take a couple hits on one of the three joints circling the table, enjoying the play of it all.

"Through one of my contacts, a well-placed black executive in the Minority Groups Development Office, I found out that they have $150,000 in excess monies. This is dough that was placed in a fund to aid in the development of an interracial group therapy program, somethin' that was supposed to help the races see eye to eye.

"O.k., now here's the kicker. The money is, was goin' to revert back to the government if such a program was not established."

He paused, checking out the gleaming eyes around him. "Of course, the Development Office couldn't openly broadcast the fact, so this is how it got to me. My well-placed black executive friend, along with a buddy of his, knew they couldn't rip off the whole one-five-oh grand. So, they put a wire out for yours truly.

"The deal we make is this; they get the small end, fifty grand, and we get the big end."

"You still ain't got into why this won't come up a lemon," Harry cut back in, more decisively.

"It won't come up a lemon, brother Harry, because my well-placed black executive friend and his friend are the one-two guys of the organization, and all they needed was an airtight proposal to approve of, to justify their approval to the Great White Father, and we got a helluva one!"

He held up the Cynthia-Chili document to clench his point. The house was suddenly bubbling over with good spirits.

Leo pulled out a pencil and began to calculate the split six ways. "Jake, why did you come up with that bullshit about mau-mauing the poverty offices 'n shit, awhile back, when

173

we first started into this?"

"That was my side tracker, baby sweets. My other thang was still in the negotiations stage, and I didn't want to breed any false hopes in the wrong directions."

"Heyyy man," Leo called out to Jake, his lips pursed, "a hundred grand between six people ain't . . . ."

"Ein is a helluva lot better than nein," Jake answered foxy quick. "A hundred grand between us may not be a fortune, but it sho' as hell beats workin'."

"How long will it take?"

"Sixty days," Jake answered promptly. "Within sixty days, we got to be lookin' like a bunch of well-established, minor league psychologists, addicted to sittin' in a circle and talkin' all the latest jargon just like the rest o' them jiveass groupsters.

"My friend ran the whole scam down to me, exactly who has to write the check out 'n everything   but just to be on the safe side, we got to have stationery 'n cards printed, a telephone, you know, stuff like that."

The group fell silent for a minute, thinking of the work to be done. Rina slowly raised her fist in the air and shouted, "All power to the Tricky Six!"

The other five people, completely in tune, responded boisterously, "All power to the Tricky Six!"

Chili mumbled under his breath . . . and my rich educated white bitch.

Kwendi and Lubertha sat looking at each other tenderly, across the glass-paneled partition. Exchanging looks and a thousand profoundly felt feelings was the way each of their visits started and ended.

"You really lookin' good, baby," Kwendi started the flow, unable to bear the weight of what the deep silence between them was saying.

"You lookin' pretty good yourself," Lubertha replied softly,

174

wishing that her spirit or some part of her being could fly across the artifical barrier between them.

The silence fell between them again, interrupted by announcements over the visiting room loudspeakers, frenetic conversations to the left and right of them, anxious people trying to say everything possible in an hour   the guards roving back and forth behind the seats of the visitors and prisoners.

"Did I tell you about what Buddha is doin' these days?" Kwendi asked brightly, always the first to try to shove them away from the emotional doldrums.

"No," Lubertha smiled back at him wistfully, her eyes straying to the summer sunlight streaming down onto them from the window at Kwendi's back.

She listened carefully to the story, alert for the coded words that might indicate he was really talking about something else. He finished the story with an attempted flourish that fell flat and looked away, trying to keep the tears from coming out of him.

"Yeah, Buddha is really something!" Lubertha commented strongly, helping him past the urge to cry. "It's too bad he doesn't write some of the lies he tells."

They both laughed cautiously, gently, as though at an old joke. Kwendi balled his fists up suddenly and pounded on his thighs, trying to massage away the tingling he felt.

"What's wrong, baby?" she asked, all love and concern.

"Ohh, nothin', nothin' really. I just been pushin' a lotta iron lately and your muscles get all tightened up sometimes doin' that, you know what I mean?"

Lubertha nodded numbly, wishing that the hour was over and wishing that it had just started, wishing that she could open her legs under the long counter and receive her man's frustrations, love him then and there.

They avoided each other's eyes for a few moments, trying

175

to reorder themselves.

Kwendi gained control of himself first and stared lustfully at the woman he loved. How many summertimes had they sat across from each other? Wanting to touch, kiss, love. How many? "Lubertha?"

She stared back at him, surprised to hear him call her that, . . . over the years he had coined the nickname, Cush, for her and had used nothing else.

"Yes?"

"Do you know how much I love you?"

A temporary attack of shyness forced her to lower her eyes. "I . . . I think so."

He opened his mouth to say more, but the guard's stick tapping him on the shoulder canceled it out. "Time's up, Jones."

They both looked at the guard in disbelief. Their time couldn't be up, they had just sat down, had just begun to talk about important things. Nothing had been said.

"I said, time's up, Jones," the guard stressed each word.

Kwendi felt the corners of his mouth pull down, his temper begin to rise.

"Be cool, baby," Lubertha said across the barrier, unable to stand up, afraid that her tension would force her legs to buckle. "Be cool, baby," she said again, as Kwendi was led away, back to his tier.

Kwendi sat on his bunk, leaning his back against the wall, feeling the pressure from his homemade knife as he leaned, brooding. Motherfuckers   He glanced apprehensively at the open cell door from time to time, thinking back to the too brief conversation he had had with Lubertha a few short hours past, about what they had said, . . . nothing. And what they would have liked to have said, everything.

My Dearest Cush, you like that, don't you? his mental let-

176

ter began. Once again summer is here and this no-longer-young man's thoughts turn to his love. I'll warn you at the beginning, everything is on my mind, so don't pay any attention to how it's put. Six brothers have been stabbed already this month, I guess the prison sap is rising a little faster this year.

He shook his head, erasing the imaginary letter, bounced from his bunk to snatch a pencil and pad from his storage shelf and remounted the bunk to write a real letter. Impulsively he began, "I'm happy about your book, so happy I don't even know how to express my feeling in words. I hope you become rich and famous (no shit!)."

He dropped the pencil and felt for the shiv stuck down in the back of his belt when he heard the footsteps.

"Writin' again, young warrior?" the Great Lawd Buddha asked him, looming up in his cell door.

Kwendi relaxed. "Yeah, bruh Buddha ... I thought I could put my time to better use than watchin' a ten year old racist flick."

"Yeah, me too, I'm deep into a book on spiders."

They smiled warmly at each other.

"Stay well," Buddha said, goin' on, "and watch your back."

"Right on!" Kwendi snapped and sat staring at the bars, the cages across the tier, after Buddha's departure.

"You know something, baby?" he continued scribbling impulsively, as though just beginning his letter disregarding all attempt at cohesion, "prison can be a strange thing. I reach a point sometimes when it seems that I don't care. Really 'n truly. Maybe it's some kind of hypnosis. I don't have a name for the feeling, but I recognize it when it comes down on me. Call it fatalism if you like.

"Awww, but that's not where I want to go. I *do* hope your book is more than a damn success, I hope it's read, especially by those ego trippers in the Club. They need a whole

177

lot more truth laid on them. Too bad they couldn't understand why you had to leave them, squabbling and ripping each other up as usual.

"I've tried to lay some weight on Abdul's head but he's so far off into being a savior that he can't relate to reason anymore. Too bad.

"Big Momma as a Muslim sister? Beautiful. I guess if Baby June could make it into the Nation, as fouled up as he was, no reason why Big Momma couldn't give up snuff Inshallah!

"Rudy got a kite through to me last week, did I tell you? Talking about his law studies, I really appreciate the help he has given on my case, but mostly it was about his feelings for Phyllisine Evans, once again, Inshallah!

"No, baby, I haven't become religious, not in that sense anyway, but Inshallah (God be willing) is a beautifully poetic expression that the Muslim brothers here use and I kinda like it.

"Onward!

"My day was made when I heard that Taco, Rina, Leo, Harry, Chili and Jake the Fake had cleaned the Office of Systematic Black Devaluation out for $300,000. The figure sounds a little high to me, but no matter, if they only beat them out of $300, at least some of that money finally reached some of the people who've had to habitually steal for a living, or worse. More power to the sisters 'n brothers!

"What fantastic times we live in. I can remember a time when those particular sisters and brothers would've never taken themselves beyond a spontaneous ripoff. Maybe having an authentic, unrehabilitated crook as the ex-vice president of the country and an outright criminal with murderous tendencies as the president of the country has been an inspiration to a lot of people."

Kwendi calmly stuck his pencil behind his ear when his

178

eye caught sight of the shadow cast by someone standing beside his cell door. He and the shadow remained in place for a few tense seconds.

Smitty, the guard, tired of the cat and mouse game, eased into view, almost causing Kwendi to pull his weapon out. "No pitcher show for you tonight, young waryer?" he asked slyly, sarcastically, peering across at the tablet on Kwendi's lap.

"Not tonight," Kwendi answered drily   creep.

"Too bad, good pitcher   lotsa action."

Kwendi straightened his back, sitting on his bunk, and gave the guard such a dignified, mean, cold, merciless look that he simply walked away without another banal word, unable to cope with what the look said to him about his mother, his father, and all of the elements that made him feel proud of being a "guard."

The hate that Smitty felt tightened him up so badly that he had to grit his teeth a few times before continuing his rounds.

"Lubertha, my beautiful Cush," Kwendi continued as soon as Smitty passed on, "why do I waste all these words and all this paper? Doing everything but recording my love for you. I should spend myself lavishly on my feelings for you with every motion the pencil makes. I should scream, rant, rave my emotions across these pages like a madman, but instead I go off into what I think of our political system.

"It smells worse every year, the ways and means to combat institutionalized racism and all the rest of the institutionalized bullshit most of us suffer under. See what I mean? Why can't I just leave my mind and heart at institutionalized loving you? And stop!

"Wish I could, sho' do. Wish I could!

"I guess if my head didn't pound as hard as my heart, if I could slide by all the hypocrisy, the sham and shuck that I see around me every day, well, I guess I wouldn't be locked

179

up, would I? Being in the inner prison, like the inner city, is a particularly good place to observe a lot of the crap from the only real problem is that the smell really gets you down sometimes.

"I meant to ask you earlier, how are your parents? Your father especially? From what you've been layin' on me, sounds like he has gone almost completely around. Groovy. I think it's almost obscene sometimes how little attention so many of today's so-called young militants have forgotten the brothers like your father.

"Who knows? Maybe I'm getting old myself, but one of the things I've learned over a period of time is how to pay closer attention to the minds of some of these gray heads.

"Let's face it, some of them got so badly brutalized so early that they are just shells, but the others, the ones who grew out from under their oppression, have something vital to say to all of us. A lot of things bother me these days, maybe it's because I have too much time to think. I'm bothered by the fake wars that are created by the rich man's media for black people to deal with, for example. Strange, isn't it? I think, that despite the fact we are a more unified people than we've ever been, there is too often an overblown story somewhere about how badly we get along.

"No matter whether it be the so-called sister-brother battle or the sister-sister battle or the brother-brother battle, or whatever. They don't overemphasize the internal problems of the Lithuanian community or the Chinese.

"Mentioning the Chinese, the yellow people. It's a shame that our people won't pay as close attention as we should to the lessons that many other peoples could teach us. The Japanese, the European Jews of Israel, the Chinese and the Scandinavians come to my mind, along with the Swiss.

"Yeahhh, I'm hip to what a lot of the brothers would probably say   It ain't black-black-black.

180

"And, I guess in the sense that they understand blackness, it wouldn't be. But I think we owe our people the best kind of life that they can have for the remainder of their time on Mother Earth. Somehow, to me, it seems stupid not to be as selective as we can possibly be about our needs   damn the Wants for awhile. We've been carefully programmed to want. Want is a luxury, not a need.

"We want a hog, we don't need one. We want a flashy wardrobe, we don't need one.

"If only we could learn a facet of the Japanese lesson. Here is the only group of people on earth that the white men experimented an atomic bomb on (they would've dropped a few on the Indians, if they'd had some), and what it did to them is something we can see happening right before our very own eyes. My theory is that their hats went so deep that they decided to take over the world that was responsible for bombing them. And, as we can see, they be doin' it too.

"I think we could learn a helluva lot from them about many economic things.

"I get so goddamned tired of hearing so much so-called black talk, darkass rhetoric is what I call it, talk designed to excite the people, and then what? I'm not saying become exactly like the Japanese, because they're fucking themselves up, becoming mechanical-computer-chrysanthemums. Remember how much I used to disagree with Rudy about his Third World approach? Well, I hate to admit it, but on quite a few points, the brother is right.

"We've been so programmed to deal with our own localized oppression that we forget that there are other people in the world in much worse shape than we're in.

"Can you imagine the kind of force we would constitute if we stretched our groovy black hands straight down south? Like, I mean, through Mexico, Central America and into South America as a whole. They have a bunch of Indian folks

181

that we could hook up with, not to mention the 'overseas' blacks, and I ain't just talking about Mother Africa either."

Cherub Brooks strolled into the cell, taking off his shirt and yawning. Kwendi felt foolish for allowing himself to be taken by surprise by his cellmate's entrance. The joint was not a hip place to allow surprises to happen. "How was the movie, bruh?" he asked, cleaning up behind his oversight.

"Shhhiit! If I'd a known they were gonna show something that fuckin' bad, I'd a stayed home and played with my dick."

Kwendi laughed, the tension gone for a few minutes.

Cherub Brooks, all five-feet-five of him, ex-boxer, ex-pimp, ex-bookie, ex-juvenile delinquent, rapist thief, drug peddler, con-man, swiveled his baby face around on his muscular, weightlifter's neck as Smitty and three other guards marched up to the door of the cell.

Kwendi high-signed to Cherub on the q.t., get this to my woman . . . and casually dropped the tablet on his bunk as he stood up.

"O.k. Jones, roll up your bedding and let's go."

"Go where, for what?"

"I'm signing you into the Hole for thirty, for insubordination."

"For whaaaa . . .?"

"You heard me, damnit! Insubordination! And I got witnesses." He nodded toward his three partners, who nodded back agreeably, shotguns leveled.

Kwendi smiled bitterly and turned to his cellmate. "See what I mean, Cherub? When I talk about revolution. There is no way to please the oppressor's strange whims, you must attempt to overthrow him by any means necessary."

Cherub looked into his friend's eyes and saw black steel shimmering.

"C'mon outta that cell, you sonavabitch! Or we'll come in and drag your black ass out, piece by piece!"

Kwendi smiled again, this time at the four beefy men standing in front of him, and suddenly charged them, the impact of his move was so sudden and so great that Smitty, Kwendi's knife in his eyebrow, and the guard next to him were falling over the tier railing before their weapons fired.

The other two guards and Cherub looked over the rail solemnly, down at the heaped trio on the stone floor, three floors below.

"That dirty rotten son of a bitch!" one of the guards muttered and leaned his shotgun against the tier railing, hostility negating his customary regard for s.o.p.

"C'mon, Moose, let's throw this bastard over too!"

The two guards immediately found themselves dealing with a man fighting and screaming for his life.

The writhing heap of men below, Kwendi, Smitty and the other guard, tangled, broken, dying   and the grunting, savage struggle going on between Cherub and the vengeful guards was enough for the mass of prisoners returning from the movies.

The newspaper headline said, two days later, in retrospect, "Riot Started By Inmate's Suicide."

Epilogue

Lubertha sat in her room, looking out at her neighborhood, at the stream that seemed to be shimmering up from it in the aftermath of a sweltering summer day. She began to slowly unbraid her hair, row by row, absently.

The funeral was over, and there was a degree of happiness mixed in with her sadness . . . At least, goddamnit! he's not behind bars, caged up like an animal anymore.

She could hear her mother and father talking quietly from the next room, the tinkle of whiskey glasses. Even her mother was having a taste. Why not get drunk after the world had come to an end?

A crooked smile flitted across her mouth as the Spinning Top Dude turned the corner and began to struggle up the street, weaving drunkenly through the groups of people congregated on the sidewalks, trying to evade the crackerbox heat of their shellshocked rooms. Bet he really misses his buddy

I bet

The sudden, agonized growl that tore itself from her throat surprised her, the angry sound of a hurt animal.

Mrs. Franklin rushed to the bedroom door. "Lubertha, you awright, baby?"

The moment gone, eroded by a steady stream of silent tears, she answered calmly. "I'm awright, Momma   I'm awright."

"Are you sure?" her mother asked, wanting to make certain, wanting to go beyond the door and nurse her daughter's grief.

"Uhhhhuh," Lubertha answered.

Mrs. Franklin walked back slowly to the front room, nodding to her man, she's all right, she's all right. They both understood that she wanted to be alone at this point in time.

Lubertha held her face in her hands for a few minutes, muffling her grief, the tears dripping like blood through her fingers. Finally, as though in a trance, she glided over to her desk, pulled ten sheets of paper from her desk drawer and began to write. "Dear Kwendi," she began, before realizing her mistake. She felt the impulse to break down completely, but held the urge back and erased the words instead.

Starting on a fresh sheet of paper, she headed it, "Lament for Kwendi."

"Lament for Kwendi

"Kwendi, a love lost, a child unborn, another bloody sacrifice. In the beginning you were there, the greatest and best impact on my eighteenth year

184

The man for all my life,
the one who understood exactly what kind of love I had to
have,   and what kind of love I had to give.
Our exchange was beautifully even steven.

Kwendi, a love found, a child unborn, another bloody
sacrifice.

We knew, soon after our spirits mated, that there was no
hope for us, just wanting justice.
But, being black, we hoped anyway.

Blindly we hoped, the disillusioned outcasts of a cynical,
racist society.

We rapped about the possibility of changing 'our country,'
this hypocritical fortress that our slave masters forced us to
call home, long ago.
No wonder, you often said, that there were no champeen black
swimmers,   who in the hell would dig swimming after
a Middle Passage Trip?

With the outside possibility of change for the better, from
every kind of bitterness, to some kind of sweetness, we formed
the Club.

It was not the first Club. The first shipment of our fore-
fathers formed the first Club
the name for an instrument that we hoped to use with constructive force.

But we were young and hadn't fully realized how well our
people's minds had been seersuckered, hogged, dogged,
slanted, catalogued, footballed, tracked, highjumped,

185

whiskied, wigged, doped, bleached

Kwendi, a love lost, a black prince unborn, an idea killed.

Yes, we were young and thought a summer of the Truth
would be enough   Stark white realities forced us to go
to other places, come out of strange bags, go to war.
We had no choice, as young and naive as we were, after we
discovered for ourselves that the police really were our
judges
the courts only had real justice for the rich
and that prisons were designed to make better criminals.

Especially black criminals, reserved cells for those who
have been taught best how to occupy them.

What did we ask for, baby?   Other than life, liberty
and the right to pursue some happiness without being
harassed.

For asking too loudly they took you prisoner.
Kwendi, my love, a stolen father, another black hostage of
the State.

Kwendi, dead now, another victim of the Lie.

The Lie, that national force that operates with negative
vibes, keeps criminals in positions of power, and tries to con-
quer us by subdividing   'Them dirty A-rabs!'
Kwendi, Kwendi, Kwendi . . . ."
Lubertha stared at Kwendi's name through her tears.
Kwendi, let's go! Kwendi, let's go! Kwendi, let's go!
The complete realizing of why he had chosen to call him-
self Kwendi fell in on her. Oh wowwww! How can I sit around

186

here writing laments for a black man who called himself "Let's go!"

She squinted at the paper and scribbled across the top of the page "No laments for Kwendi."